Uncle John's Bedtime Tales.

by

John Vault

Spinetinglers publishing.

Spinetinglers Publishing
22 Vestry Road, Co. Down
BT23 6HJ, UK
www.spinetinglerspublishing.com

First published by Spinetinglers Publishing, March 2011.

ISBN: 978-1-906755-19-5

Printed in the United Kingdom

This work is dedicated to Gail, the love of my life.
Special thanks to Jeff, for his sharp eyes and blunt honesty.

Cover by Eleanor.

Contents.

Introduction.

If you're looking for vampires, werewolves and all things nocturnal turn back now, because there are none in these pages.

Modern horror and dark fiction fans have stepped up their expectations. The horror icons that scared the wits out of our grand parents in silvery monochrome all those years ago are now the subjects of modern television romance, having been pimped with beautiful faces and chiselled, Greek god physiques.

The visions of blood and gore that once solicited ear splitting screams are no more now than the filler between sex scenes, and having had our senses drenched in these we are immune to them. So let us cast them aside and ask the question, what really scares us?

I don't know what scares you, but I know what scares me, which is why the tales in this book are loosely based around a common theme...

Madness.

Why madness? Because it's real. Because even you dear reader, have the potential to slip between the friendly fingers of sanity and plummet into the darkly splendid world of lunacy and obsession. For many of you it's already waiting, just a little way out of sight, in the shadowy spaces between your everyday thoughts. You wouldn't even see it coming.

So, if you relish the prospect of dipping a toe into the icy cold and dreadfully dark waters of insanity to

i

see if you come back unchanged, then these bedtime tales are for you.

In this book there are strange people in terrifying circumstances.

There are buckets of blood, graveyards, old houses and horrific dreams. There are twisted tales of obsession where no-one is who or what they seem.

What there may not be however, is a particularly good night's sleep.

Enjoy.

John V.

Tiw's Cup.

The mist was lifting, leaving only the bitter cold behind. It bit into his face with icicle teeth as he drew a deep breath and turned his stiffened neck to look around him. He couldn't remember anything, not even his name.

Ethan, his own voice eventually told him. His name was Ethan.

Ethan sat, his back propped up against the mouldering dampness of the wall. The half light revealed something of his surroundings. An old room, empty and smelling of rot. Wires hung out of the walls like burst veins. Floorboards, dry like old bones. The windows dusty and pock marked with brick holes placed by the young engaged in dismantling the old.

And all this blood.

The survival instinct is a singular entity. Ethan didn't care where the blood had come from, only that it wasn't his. He felt no pain and was therefore gently reassured.

The mist lifted further. Ethan sat for a short eternity between thoughts. His body, rigid and heavy, felt no inclination to move. This pale mist, an odd composition of thickness and light felt almost tangible to him. In normal circumstances thick fog allows you to see that which is close up but obscures the distance. This mist, which filled the room,

3

seemed to work the opposite way around. But it was lifting, Ethan felt sure. It was only a matter of time.

His cold mind though still somewhat solid and lethargic forced his eyes to rest on his bare feet. At least he assumed that they were his. These were dirty and misshapen, bulbous and swollen, but they seemed to be in the right place so they must be his. Damn this fucking fog! Where the hell was he?

This question was not uncommon in Ethan's life. Anyone else would have had grave cause for concern if they had been in a situation that prompted this question more than a few times in their entire span. But in Ethan's life this question came up a lot! Ethan was an adventurer, a spiritual warrior, a Byronic hero. Waking up in strange places with no memory of the previous night was what he did.

From an early age he'd been considered intellectually gifted. He could speak intelligibly at six months old and read pretty much anything by the age of four. His parents positively celebrated him but they were inevitably missing something. He was beyond them in virtually every aspect by the time he was nine. That's not to say that Ethan was arrogant or dismissive, far from it. He loved his parents deeply but his inner nature drew him into fundamental conflict with their orderly lifestyle.

He wasn't going to university. There would be no PhD. No scientific breakthrough or miracle surgery. No concert pianist or prime minister.

Ethan had decided to live instead.

They had accepted his decision in grave silence, and their unvoiced disappointment had torn him down more effectively than all the anger, tears and emotional blackmail that they could have used had they loved him less than they did.

There was so much in the world to be appreciated and Ethan was spiritually inspired to appreciate it. He'd left home at eighteen with a rucksack and two hundred pounds. He'd picked a road at random and stuck out his thumb.

There had been women on his travels. He was known by name in almost every brothel in Europe it seemed. He'd shagged his way around the world, eaten every conceivable delicacy, stood atop mountains and drunk the oceans dry.

And then of course there were the drugs. Opium in China, hashish in Morocco, peyote in Mexico, LSD in San Francisco. You name it; Ethan had snorted, swallowed, smoked, popped, sniffed, chased or mainlined it. He had screamed into the face of God after drinking Virola juice in Columbia and awakened ten days later emaciated and caked with shit, strapped to a stinking, bug ridden mattress in a far away hovel. He'd almost died of dysentery.

What a fucking rush.

But what if anything, had he learned? Ethan was quick but he still never quite figured it out. The big lesson, that hedonism dulls the senses. You can only take so many stimuli before the brain begins to close down and ignore them. So to get the same buzz you have to go further, take more, and do more.

So he did.

Spiritual greed is greed nonetheless. His body had suffered. At twenty seven he looked like a man of fifty. Only his eyes betrayed his true age. They burned in their darkened sockets like emerald flares. He would not live a long life. But it would be a life to make the Gods envious.

At the peak of his own self destruction he'd been sitting, or rather slumping in a bar in Reykjavik, listening to a silver bearded academic piss head rattling on about how the Viking invasions of Western Europe were still affecting world politics. His Absinthe glass was empty, this made him sad.

'If we still had it', the piss head slurred, 'we could rule the world.'

Ethan picked his forehead up from the table.

'Had what?'

'Tiw's cup.' Piss head belched. 'Tiw's fokking cup!'

'What?'

'The Berserkers.' Piss head's eyes rolled in their sockets. 'The Viking warriors, feared by everyone. They drink from Tiw's cup and go completely fokking insane. They run into battle naked and kill everything that moves. The recipe was lost. If we still had it....' His voice trailed off, his drunken stupor victorious.

Sometimes the smallest of things are significant. The discarded cigarette that begets the forest fire. The irritating glint in the foaming rapids that entices the salmon to the hook.

Ethan was caught. His bored spirit had found new hope in the small promise of a stone yet unturned. It stirred once again engaging the help of his rusty but still remarkable intellect. He spent the next few months in libraries, museums and internet cafes looking for references to the magical brew known as Tiw's cup. He found manuscripts, extracts and historical notes that pushed him into lateral avenues of folk lore, botany and neurochemistry. There were new languages and dialects to absorb, places to go, people to see. Ethan's life turned around.

It took four years, but in the end a small sheet of paper held the sum of his relentless enquiries. He had it, 'Tiw's Cup', the recipe for divine madness. The ingredients were surprisingly easy to obtain. Common sense dictated that they had to be freely available throughout Western Europe. Psilocybe mushrooms formed the basic juice, Lobelia, Wormwood and Lopium followed although the quantities varied with each account, throw in a little Hemlock and garnish with a pinch of ergot of rye. There seemed to be no real complexity involved. The reason for this was simple. It didn't work. He'd locked himself away in a hostel room and thrown the key out of the window because he didn't want to risk hurting anyone. Having cooked it all up he downed it in one gulp, wincing at its bitterness. He'd buzzed for the next six hours, had a few strange visions, laughed until his ribs ached, vomited liberally and then fallen asleep. All in all it was nothing that he hadn't done many times before.

There had to be some missing ingredient or at least an aspect of the preparation that formed a catalytic effect. For weeks he returned to his precious photocopies. Manuscripts, legends and the odd learned dictation formed the core of his research. After hundreds of ever decreasing mental circles there was one in the end that threw him a lifeline.

A photocopy of a single historical reference which at first glance had seemed too superficial to be of any importance, but being the man that he was he had copied it anyway. The key it seemed was in the phrasing. It said simply 'the drink was made for each warrior...' at least that's the way he'd interpreted it. Ethan wasn't that hot on the use of redundant Scandinavian possessive terms. This implied that the brew was customised to suit the individual. But how the hell was that supposed to happen? He threw the papers down and sat in silence. Ethan's intellect, powerful as it was, seemed lost. As his thoughts ground slowly to a halt a small light went on somewhere inside him and in the silence his heart screamed the answer.

Blood.

When he'd drunk the virola juice the shaman who made it told him to breathe into the mixture otherwise it wouldn't work because the spirits of the tree wouldn't recognise him. Ethan had laughed, but blown into the pot anyway. He knew nothing of spirits, he just wanted the buzz.

He'd read various accounts of druids and witches using blood to bind potions to specific people. It was common practice in medieval medicine and in some

7

areas of the world it still is. There was a downside of course, the risk of severe allergic reaction. Everything's fine the first time you take it, but take it again and you're dead. The problem is that you don't know whether you've reacted or not until it's too late.

He knew he was right this time. He felt it with the firm certainty that always accompanied the solution to a difficult problem. He would make the potion again but this time he would add his own blood.

Over the next few days Ethan had found a more suitable venue for his grand experiment. He'd been out in a small patch of woodland hunting amongst the roots of the old birch for Psilocybe mushrooms. The September weather had put a thick layer of mud and leaves on his already distressed training shoes and the clothing that he habitually wore, jeans and a loose fitting sweater, were proving of little help against the cold damp air. As it started to rain he'd looked up from his quest to find shelter. He'd noticed the old house then, set back amongst the thickest part of the wood. It had been well and truly abandoned though Ethan could barely imagine why such a formerly grandiose place had been left to decay. Perhaps the owner had more money than sense.

On closer inspection the house proved to be empty as Ethan had suspected although still quite secure it seemed. This would be a good place. Quiet and secluded, away from everyone and any possibility of disturbance. And if he became sick well he'd just have to deal with it. A bottle of brine was guaranteed to empty his stomach within minutes if needed. He'd bring some with him.

He'd returned to the house two days later. It was twilight and the air was cold. He'd already prepared the brew minus the blood. He'd brought a razor blade for that job. Ethan wasn't fond of pain but sometimes you have to make sacrifices.

Unfortunately he'd found the house to be more secure than he'd initially estimated but there was an outhouse around the side that may have something in it that he could use to pry open a window. As luck would have it he found an old toolbox which held various bits and pieces that were perfect for a spot of breaking and entry.

Having levered open a small window he climbed inside. The smell of mildew greeted him as he sneaked into the hallway looking for the stairs. This house could be safely categorised as spooky or possibly borderline creepy. His mind flicked back to his childhood, watching TV with his parents. Tales of mystery and imagination. 'Not for people of a nervous disposition' the announcer had said every week before the program began. Talk about the power of suggestion. That single phrase had scared him far more profoundly than the incredulous rubbish that had followed for the next hour. Ethan chuckled to himself as he mounted the dark staircase. Adrenalin was already focussing his attention on the slightest of movements.

He checked out the bathroom. No water, just grime on the mildewed shower curtain and puss coloured lime scale where the bath tap had once dripped. There were dead flies on the windowsill and hanging by the legs from the rotting lace curtain. The toilet bowl was dry and coated with dirt but at least he'd have somewhere to shit and puke should the need arise.

The bedrooms were next. Each one was much the same as the others with its high ceilings ornate with intricate plaster covings and pale squares on the walls where pictures had once hung. He chose the one nearest the bathroom; it was as good as any. The window overlooked a small roof that would serve as an escape route if needed. He tried to open it but found his strength insufficient for the task. He went back downstairs for the toolbox and having loosened the reluctant sash frame he put the tools away in the corner.

He fished two tee light candles from the pocket of his jeans and placed them on the floor. He lit each one carefully with a dark blue disposable lighter that he'd carried around for months. He had to tilt the lighter right over to get to the short wick and he cursed aloud as he burned a finger on the tiny yellow flame. The house seemed to shudder at his voice as if sound itself had become a thing long forgotten.

As each of the tee lights warmed through their flames grew slightly brighter and the room became alive with dancing shadows and although they couldn't possibly have had any significant effect on the temperature of the room Ethan would have sworn that he felt warmer and more comfortable.

He sighed heavily and the flames flickered and the shadows danced. He reached into his other pocket and retrieved a small jar. He was glad to take it out because it had been digging into his hip as he moved. He'd no idea of the dosage required or how much blood he'd have to put in. Perhaps only a few drops would suffice, perhaps not. He unscrewed the lid of the jar and placed both jar and lid carefully on the floor between the candles. He reached into his back pocket to claim the razor blade which he'd wrapped in several layers of paper. He unwrapped the blade and it glinted in the pale candlelight.

Holding his left hand over the open jar he approached the base of his thumb with the blade. He hesitated, unable to make the cut. He cursed his own cowardice.

'It's just subconscious self defence.' he assured himself. 'Just make the fucking cut.'

He swiped at his hand hoping to somehow cut himself by accident. Oddly enough this actually worked although he had to keep pinching the pitifully shallow wound to milk the liquid out. He managed two drops, watching each one adopt the shape of a swirling toroid as it penetrated the relatively clear liquid in the jar. He stirred it in with his finger.

So then, this was it. He raised the jar as if making a toast. He imagined for a moment that Tiw the Norse war god had opened a lazy eye to witness an event not enacted for over a thousand years. A mild shiver played along Ethan's spine.

'Tiw,' he spoke aloud, 'it's been a while. Can you still do it?'

He gulped down half of the brew. At least two of the ingredients were potentially lethal so if he survived the next hour he'd consider drinking the rest then. He sat back and waited.

Twenty minutes elapsed. Ethan became impatient, then frustrated. But something was happening. Nothing special, just his heartbeat, slowing but becoming harder, almost audible. Some of the alkaloids in the brew were depressants so it was no great shock that his cardiac rhythm was affected. But it was loud, very loud, fearfully loud. His vision grew foggy, as if a mist had descended on the place. He expected more, flashing lights, voices perhaps, but nothing materialised and after a while the beat of his heart subsided. His disappointment turned to desperation as he picked up the jar and threw the remaining brew to the back of his throat. He slammed the jar against the wall where it exploded into twinkling fragments. Hitting the floorboards hard with his fist he swore into the empty room.

His knuckles, grazed by the impact, began to sting but this sensation was short lived and quickly replaced by something else, something totally out of context and unexpected.

Pleasure.

A warm, relaxed and almost orgasmic sensation sprouted from his injured hand and expanded out towards his elbow. But it didn't stop there. It reached his shoulder, increasing in intensity, almost burning.

'Fucking hell!' Ethan gasped. His body grew hotter, his skin felt inflamed, irritated. Soon the heat became unbearable. He tore at his clothes, scratching at the flesh of his stomach as he pulled at his sweater. Again the orgasmic wave began. Sprouting from the scratches, pouring into his loins and down his legs. 'Shit, shit, fucking Jesus shit!' Ethan pulled off the rest of his clothes. He had to get naked, to cool off or he'd explode. He stood motionless in the cold darkness, totally internalised. He knew what this was.

Sensory transference. It was common enough with LSD. The brain confused the sensory input streams and misinterpreted everything. You could see sounds as colours and hear colours as tones. Pictures and words became the same thing mingled and indistinguishable. But this was different. Pain into pleasure? He slapped himself across the face and the wave started immediately. Blasts of hysterically intense sensations pushed into the nerve roots in his teeth and ears, flashing like lightening in his mind's eye. Ethan became ecstatic. Laughing manically he slapped himself again, caving in and falling to his knees under the relentless pressure of orgasm after orgasm. His knees hit the floor and pleasure burst forth like liquid fire engulfing his testicles. He could sell this stuff. He would be seriously fucking rich.

He dropped forwards onto all fours. His skin was reddened and he was sweating profusely. As his hands touched the floor the waves started, immersing his head and neck in spasmodic jolts of ferocious pleasure. So it wasn't just pain that triggered the pleasure response Ethan noted. It was any tactile sensation at all. A sickness fell upon him as he crouched in the darkness. A side effect of the Lobelia. His stomach heaved but nothing came up and as his abdomen cramped the wave sprouted again. This time it washed him away.

'Fuck this is good.' Ethan groaned, barely able to hold himself up. He reached for a piece of the broken jar and with some hesitance jabbed it into his thigh. The pleasure wave hit him so hard that he lost control of his bowel. But it wasn't the same as before. A different type of pain generates a different sensation of pleasure. Slaps and bangs were good but cuts, Ethan thought to himself, cuts were totally fucking groovy! He jabbed the glass shard into the same wound and then twisted it. He howled and fell, rolling onto his back and giggling hysterically. He shit himself again and then ejaculated. Breathing hard he rolled his head back and forth on the floorboards feeling the powerful pleasure response now subtle in comparison to the electrifying jolts leaping from his gushing thigh. He watched his blood expand across the dusty floor caring nothing for it. Then he caught sight of something that may as well have been the Holy Grail.

'Oh yes.' Ethan laughed. 'Come to daddy.' It took approximately seven orgasms to reach the toolbox but it was going to be worth the effort.

Ethan giggled, heaving open the rusted lid. He picked out a large hammer, nodding his approval. He splayed his hand out on the floor and slammed the hammer down hard on his index finger. He collapsed instantly, all his strength blasted away by a pleasure so intense that he would have cheerfully died right there. He gathered himself up and hit it again and again.

'Fight it Ethan,' he moaned 'you can take this shit all fucking day.' He launched a frenzied attack on the rest of his fingers but in the end it still wasn't enough. Hedonism dulls the senses. He kept hitting though just to make sure, right up until he spotted the pliers.

John Vault

He reasoned carefully as he picked the heavy
rusted grips out of the box. If busting a finger sent
him to heaven then pulling a tooth should fire him
straight up almighty God's arse and out of his
mouth. He chose a large molar. At least then nobody
would notice the gap. His plan misfired, but in a
good way. Instead of gripping the tooth and working
it loose he squeezed too hard and the tooth shattered.
His eyes rolled back and his arms fell limp at his
sides. He knelt for a while in a pool of hot urine
convulsing softly. When he finally became lucid he
went straight for another molar but something
inside him shouted fuck it and in a twenty second
flurry he smashed every tooth in his head and begun
grinding the stumps together while choking on the
pieces. He did indeed fly up God's arse.

Having no more teeth left him at something of an
impasse. What he wouldn't have given for a litre of
boiling water and a rubber tube. Then he
remembered the razor blade.

'Cuts are good.' he reminded himself, 'Cuts are our
friends.'

The veins and arteries run longitudinally, Ethan
remembered from secondary school biology, so
cutting across lost you more blood per inch of
incision than slicing up and down. Feeling smug at
his reasoning he picked the silver edged blade from
the blood crusted floor and ran it lightly down the
inside of his left thigh. The pleasure wave was
initially sharp but quickly died off and then slowly
built to a more acceptable intensity. Ethan was
disappointed. He wanted an explosion. After waiting
a little longer he put the blade in the same wound
and dug deep. The explosion came, pushing him
beyond pleasure and into transcendence. Floating
freely amongst the gods for an eternity made instant
Ethan was truly at one with all things. He would
have stayed there. He would have died a thousand
horrific deaths for one more second but the gods

14

drew back, and as they abandoned him he wept. A weakness overtook him. He inspected the wound in his leg through tearful eyes. His femoral artery was open and his life was pouring out, spreading like a scarlet vine at his feet.

He lurched over to where his clothes lay and scooped up his jeans. Ripping the thin leather belt from the loops he wrapped it around his thigh at the groin and jerked it tight. He stood swaying in the dim candle light. There was fear. There was dread. There was realisation.

The magic was failing. The potion was wearing off. He wanted more.

Ethan wanted to live amongst the gods again. He'd worked hard for it. He deserved it. To be away from them, only that was death.

He screamed, kicking at the walls and cracking the ancient plaster away, the bones of his toes shattered under the impact. Not enough.

He punched the windows. The skin of his forearms peeled and the tendons split and shrank back. Not enough.

Each remorseless act bore waves of pleasure that died away like birth strangled children.

This was the moment that the berserker became. Not in the gaining of his power, but at the loss of it. Screaming and crying Ethan bowed his head and ran at the nearest wall. The cracking of his skull echoed through the cold dark house. He finally fell, unconscious to the floorboards.

Several hours later, as daylight hinted at the possibility of its arrival, Ethan awoke.

***

The mist was lifting and now Ethan knew the truth. Soon the magic of Tiw's cup would be completely gone and he'd be cast into a world of unimaginable pain. He reached down slowly and deliberately to untie the thin leather tourniquet from his thigh and as the fount of his life spewed forth Ethan thought that he may be lucky after all.

What a fucking rush.

*****

John's Story.

A single spotlight picked him out. Too bright for the eyes and harsh against the dim shadows of the stage, he seemed to be composed of little more than varying degrees of white.

The students filed in, white clad and bejewelled with silver stethoscopes that represented office rather than experience. Each one turned to a colleague to whisper as they caught sight of him. The auditorium was filling rapidly but no-one chose to occupy the front row of seats.

Each student picked up the lecture notes that had been positioned at their place along the dark brown heavily marked wooden tables. Some struggled to read them in the half light while others just carried on talking in hushed tones, but all were aware of him and all were uneasy.

It was a perhaps a further fifteen minutes before one of them began to voice her concern at him being left there, alone and unattended for so long. She stood up; a shadow amongst shadows.

'Are you alright?' She asked. He didn't respond. 'Do you need anything?'

'I'm afraid you're wasting your time,' a strong and resonant voice sounded from the side of the stage accompanied by sharp footsteps, 'He's completely unaware of your presence, and of his own for that matter.' A tall pale man in a dark blue pinstripe suit walked briskly into the edge of the spotlight. He raised a hand to block out its brightness and peered out into the audience. 'That's Miss Ellis isn't it? If I'm not mistaken. Please sit down, all will be revealed.'

He looked toward the back of the lecture theatre as the last chink of light from the corridor was severed by the closing of the door.

'So we're all in then, and a good turn out it seems. I'm aware that you are all at different stages of your journey through our fine institution and that some of you won't yet appreciate the subtler points of what you're about to see, but this is a special occasion and one which both you and I are unlikely to witness again in the entire span of our respective careers. But I'm getting ahead of myself, so I'll start again where I meant to.'

He moved off to one side to occupy a small lectern. At the sound of a click a tiny light appeared over his lecture notes. A further click initiated the appearance of a large white screen that descended slowly from the back of the stage.

'As some of you will already know I am professor Robert Mason, head of psychiatric studies here at the university teaching hospital. I'd like now to introduce the subject of today's lecture, Doctor John Dante, who is I believe one of the worlds few truly catatonic human beings.'

A soft ripple of voices ran back and forth throughout the theatre as all eyes fell upon the spotlighted figure in the wheelchair. John sat, shoulders hunched, hands clawed. His pale grey gown barely concealed the angular structure of his wasted body. His right shoulder was wet with the constant sliver of drool that strung from the corner of his slack mouth. His head, which was close shaven and littered with electrodes and various coloured wires, tilted atop a twisted neck, while his glazed pale blue eyes stared at nothing.

'Oh yes', Mason continued, 'John was formerly a man of considerable achievement in several arenas. He was my friend and colleague for many years having taught as professor of forensic pathology in this very room. He was, until approximately eight months ago an officer for the district coroner when he first began to exhibit symptoms, although he was already very ill by then.'

Mason shuffled his notes and coughed lightly.

'Right then, we'll begin with a look at the basic symptoms and then we'll try to define a cause and look at appropriate care and please pay attention because this is an interactive session. I'll be expecting some input from you.' His audience sat upright in unison.

'At this stage of his illness John sees, hears and feels absolutely nothing. He has no inclination to move, cannot feed or clean himself and will not respond to any external stimuli. He does have the very basic reflexive motions in place however but even these are rapidly degrading. Mr. Thompson, if you will...'

A technician appeared from the shadows of the stage armed with a small feather which he gently stroked across the cornea of John's right eye. John blinked.

'That's about as exciting as it gets,' Mason grinned, 'so we make him as comfortable as possible. He's undergone a colostomy and has been catheterised. He's fed intravenously from the bags that you can see suspended on frames around his chair. He has a TV in his room but I think that it's more for our peace of mind than his. His body continues to atrophy of course and he's developing regular pressure wounds and emphysema.'

Various unintelligible whispers sprang up amongst the students.

'So, now it's your turn. Can anyone suggest a possible cause for Doctor Dante's condition? Come on, don't be shy.'

A small voice floated up from the back of the room. 'Brain metastasis?'

'Good effort but wrong.' Mason smiled. 'All scans were clear of tumours and cysts.'

'Prion disease or Alzheimer's?' Came another suggestion.

'Highly improbable due to the rapidity of onset and the complete lack of symptoms prior to first presentation. He was also capable of passing every known test for the illnesses while lucid. The cause is not pathological, that is to say, there is no physical disease or injury present that would suggest these symptoms. The cause is purely psychological. I know this because I have witnessed the development of his illness. Let me give you a few pointers.'

Mason came out from behind the lectern and paced back and forth on the stage as he spoke.

'You cannot look at him as he is and try to assess the nature of his condition. There are no psychological symptoms now because his personality is completely absent. You have to go back in time and look at how he behaved, what he did and said and how he reacted to everyday situations. So what questions do we ask?'

'What were the first symptoms?' A female voice murmured.

'YES!' Mason pointed at the voice. 'Well done Miss Ellis. We need to be aware of his initial conditions because these are the first manifestation of the root issue.'

He stood a while in thought, composing words.

'I was first made aware of John's case on the day following his initial emotional collapse. He'd been sectioned under mental health act and referred to the local psychiatric unit for assessment. When I met him he'd been sedated but was still highly agitated and tearful. We have to understand that these emotional states are not symptoms of the illness but the subject's response to those symptoms. We have to try to get past his responses to see the cause. Of course, the kind of response exhibited will often provide clues as to where to begin. In John's case he was showing signs of severe distress, the kind that stems from extraordinary levels of sustained mental trauma.'

Mason walked back to his lectern and pulled out the small sliding shelf that contained a keyboard and a mouse. At the press of a key the screen at the back of the stage flickered dimly to life.

'The document that you are about to see relates to the last case that John was working on before his collapse.' The screen flickered again, displaying a single sheet of text. 'It concerns an investigation into the death of a young lady named Susan Holland. I would draw your attention to the entry at the bottom of the form regarding the cause of death.'

After a brief pause the auditorium erupted into rapid discussion accompanied by the shaking of heads and the rustling of notes. A single word described the cause of death...

Autopsy.

Mason stood in thought for a while and then raised his hands.

'In case there are any people here who have failed to grasp the significance of this document, please allow me to spell it out.'

The audience fell silent.

'Doctor John Dante had just carried out a full post mortem examination on a young woman, a procedure that he's performed on hundreds of prior occasions. In this case however he did it under the bizarre belief that she was still very much alive.'

The silence held fast, peppered occasionally by half concealed whispers.

21

'But it doesn't end there I'm afraid because as I said earlier, John had been ill for quite some time before the initial presentation. Subsequent interviews revealed that he was burdened with the accumulated guilt from perhaps sixty previous and completely imagined murders, all by disembowelment.'

He walked back to centre stage.

'It has been said that the insane man is one who, in normal circumstances, responds abnormally. This however is only a half truth because it fails to appreciate the subject's perspective, that is, we cannot know what the patient is experiencing. Who is to say that upon stepping into his shoes, we of supposedly sound mind would not behave in exactly the same way? In my experience the profoundly disturbed person will usually exhibit quite normal responses once his subjective environment is revealed. It is his world that is different to ours. That is the issue.

So let's take this premise and use it as a tool of analysis. Let's look into John's world and see if we can make sense of his clinical development. Firstly, let us imagine each one of us, that we are John. You are forty two years old and enjoying a stable, well paid and respected career, having been afforded a privileged public school education by doting parents. Your father was an officer in the army medical corps and you have travelled with him up to the age of thirteen throughout Europe and the Middle East. You have no criminal history whatsoever and may be considered to be quite wealthy by usual standards. You are unmarried although heterosexual and are happy to live the bachelor lifestyle.'

Mason walked back to his keyboard. The screen cleared and refreshed with grainy moving images. An interview room; empty apart from a single table where Mason and John sat opposite each other. All

22

recording equipment was concealed behind one way glass panelling and a microphone was hidden in the shade of the overhead light.

Barely recognisable, John slumped at the table, head in hands. He was a little on the plump side, his rear fastening hospital gown looked tight around his shoulders and chest. He had a full head of brown hair that stuck out in sparse clumps between his fingers.

'...Michael Latham. He was the first, about a year ago.' He rubbed his hands together and scratched at the skin of his wrists as if trying to dig out a stain. Mason shuffled through the small pile of notes and transcripts on the table in front of him.

'It says here John that Michael Latham died of coronary heart disease. You wrote this yourself.' He spoke with artificial, almost patronising softness. John's body seemed to jerk as if poked with a stick. He adopted a half curled position on his chair.

'I was just lucky that's all.' John sniffed. 'The level of arterial blockage had already put him on borrowed time and the ventricular walls were discoloured due to oxygen starvation. I put it as the cause of death. There's no way on earth that anyone would have disagreed.' He squirmed slightly and hugged himself around the chest. 'But it wasn't like that. He was the first case of the day. It was eight thirty in the morning when I pulled him from the cold room. He was a young man, early thirties, who'd supposedly died in his sleep. His notes showed that apart from chicken pox at the age of six he'd enjoyed robust health.'

'But how do you account for the fact that an ambulance crew and all attending medical staff failed to notice that he was alive?' Mason interrupted. 'Although the cause of death may have been speculative at that time the fact remains that one of them surely would have noticed something.'

'I don't know!' John spat. 'Do you think I haven't thought about it? God, I've been jumping through hoops for months trying to figure it out.'

'Of course,' Mason whispered, 'I'm sorry John, please continue. You were telling me about Michael Latham.'

'I put him on the examination table and began the visual assessment. He had no unusual marks or wounds, nothing to suggest impact or penetration.' John paused, staring at the floor. The silence seemed to draw everything into it. 'It was when I turned away to get my scalpel for the visceral examination... he spoke to me.'

'He actually spoke to you?' Mason leaned forward.

'He said "No".'

'Did you see his mouth move? Were his eyes open?' Mason stared.

'I wasn't looking at him when it happened. I turned to him but he was just lying still. I thought it must be some kind of joke or something. I touched his face. It was cold. I pushed it from my mind and carried on. Anyway if it had been some kind of sick joke it would end as soon as the scalpel came into play. I put it over his left collar bone to incise across the chest. I waited for a moment to give him a chance to come clean.' John paused again.

'And then?' Mason pressed. There was no answer. 'John, you've got to tell me what happened. It's the only way I can help you.' John looked up. Tears streamed from his eyes, his mouth distorted, fighting back pain.

'Well what do you think happened?' He sobbed quietly. 'I pushed the blade into his skin, about half an inch and... he screamed.' John gulped loudly. 'God, how he screamed. I fell back against the instrument trolley. I'd never felt so sick. I grabbed a paper towel to stop the bleeding but there was no blood. Just his voice begging me to stop, and the screams. Then I did something stupid... I put my hand over his mouth.'

'Why?'

'To stop him screaming. It was absurd I know but I kept telling him. "You're dead. You have to be quiet and let me do my job." But he wouldn't listen. He begged and cried and pleaded. I carried on through the madness of it all. I had to work with one hand over his mouth. It stopped in the end, when I opened a hole into his ribcage. You can't scream with collapsed lungs. He managed another ten seconds or so, probably held on with parallax breathing. But in the end he died...'

The screen went blank and there was silence in the theatre. Mason spoke from the lectern.

'So there is John's version of the events surrounding the initial presentation of his delusional state. As you can see he has a very clear memory of the details surrounding the case. He was able to recall dates, times and chronological order accurately and consistently even though we went over the same incident several times during the interview. Apparently, according to John, it's like losing your virginity or remembering where you were the day Elvis died. You never forget your first murder.' Uneasy laughter flickered through the audience as Mason walked to centre stage.

'So let's get back inside his head shall we? By normal standards John is enjoying a privileged lifestyle. The question is then, how far would you go to protect that lifestyle? John now believes wholeheartedly that he is a murderer and that he will soon be discovered. His immediate priority therefore is to conceal his crime. This is the act of a rational person. He invented a feasible cause of death and filed the appropriate documentation, cleaned up the crime scene and carried on as usual. It is normal procedure to record post mortem examinations as they occur since the officer carrying out the examination is unable to take notes at the time. Transcripts are then produced from the recordings. In all of the cases where John claims to have committed murder these recordings were missing. The point that I'm making here is that by hiding his crime John is behaving in a logical manner, even though the initial premise that prompted his behaviour is completely absurd. I'd like you now to watch this next clip, recorded two months after the first one that you saw. John's drug regime and therapy schedule are in your notes.'

The screen flashed into life showing the same room as before. John, although somewhat slimmer than in his first appearance, and now wearing blue Jeans and a pale grey cotton shirt, seemed very relaxed.

'So how are you today John?' Mason asked.

'Not bad Robert.' John half smiled. 'Looking forward to a little time out of the grounds I think.'

'Are you anxious at all, about going outside?'

'No, not really.' John shrugged. 'It's all been a bit of a nightmare. The sooner I'm back to normal the better.'

'Good. When do you see yourself going back to work?'

'Well, as soon as possible, but I won't be going back into the autopsy business. I don't want to risk a relapse. Perhaps it was just nature's way of saying that I'm not cut out for it after all. There's plenty of lab work I can do. I won't starve.'

'So it's just out for the day initially is it?' Mason prompted.

'Yes. I did a supervised trip last week. I'm out on my own at nine a.m. Saturday and back here for seven thirty the same evening. I plan to make sure that the house is clean and secure and then visit some close friends.'

'Good,' Mason smiled. 'I'll see you when you get back and we'll talk about how it went.'

'Thank you.' John grinned.

The screen went blank.

'It seems odd doesn't it that after such a remarkable level of mental trauma John is here just a few weeks later behaving as if nothing's happened.' Mason moved closer to the edge of the stage as if drawing the audience into his confidence. 'Let me offer you a single piece of advice that will set you up for the rest of your career. Never, ever underestimate the intelligence or resourcefulness of a patient. I have to admit that I was fooled. I was arrogant enough to believe that I had all the answers and John, realising this, led me to believe that I had helped him.'

Mason walked to the lectern and once again the screen flashed.

Groans rang out across the auditorium spattered with gasps of shock. Some students turned their heads away while others put hands to their mouths. Some just stared in disbelief.

The screen showed John unconscious, naked and laid out on a hospital trolley. A gaping incision reached across his chest at the collar bones, exposing yellow adipose tissue and the contrasting blood stained whiteness of bone. A second cut extended down from the top of his sternum to his pubic bone. Coils of blue intestine poked through at intervals, hanging off his midsection like fat leeches.

One young lady left her seat and ran for the door.

'Oh God I'm so sorry!' Mason whined. 'I should've told you... I should've warned you.' He pressed a key and the picture vanished.

Mason sighed deeply and composed himself.

'He left the hospital as planned on the Saturday morning. He was in intensive care two hours later. By tremendous good fortune the friend that he planned to visit had decided to meet him at his house. How he survived this atrocious self injury I'll never know. This is when he had the colostomy. He'd

27

managed to irreparably damage his bowel with a craft knife.'

Mason took his handkerchief from his jacket pocket and wiped small beads of sweat from his forehead.

'Most criminals never get to this stage of adjustment. They just evade capture until the last possible moment. In John's case he'd already owned up to his imagined crimes and was ready to make amends with society. His problem became then that society didn't believe him to be guilty. On the contrary, instead of making him pay for his grotesque behaviour it patted him on the head and said 'There there, don't worry we'll make it alright.' John's burden of guilt therefore increased to the point where he felt that had to make atonement on his own behalf. To him nothing short of suffering the same fate as his victims would suffice. But he couldn't do that under the supervision of the hospital staff so he wilfully subdued his symptoms and behaved obligingly as if he were cured. Then of course as soon as our backs were turned, well, you've seen the rest.'

He turned once again to his lectern, speaking as he operated both mouse and keyboard.

'I have a final film clip for you to see. It occurs six weeks after John's self harming episode. He was rapidly losing the will to live at this time. Most of his day was spent sleeping and he ate very little. There was virtually nothing that anyone could do to lift his depression. Despite the extended drug therapy John's emotional state had continued to decline.'

The screen flashed, showing the interview room. John sat back in his chair, occasionally wiping the tears from his eyes with the sleeve of his gown.

'My memory of the event isn't clear. I remember being dropped off at home. I went inside, it smelled a little damp, you know what it's like when you leave a house unheated for any length of time.' He sighed deeply. 'Anyway, I put the heating on and then went to make myself a coffee. I was in the kitchen when she called.'

'By she, you mean Susan?' Mason interrupted.

'Yes.' John sniffed. 'I just froze to the spot. She was calling me into the bedroom. I don't know why. I followed her voice, it sounded frail but so insistent. I couldn't ignore it. That's when I saw her, just standing there.'

'You actually saw her?'

'Yes. She looked like she did when I killed her. She was naked. Her skin was pale blue and she had the longitudinal cut. Her breasts were peeled back off her ribcage, hanging down around her sides. Her abdomen was wide open and she was struggling to gather up her entrails in her arms and push them back inside. They were sliding through her hands. God, she looked so desperate. She just kept looking at me. She was crying and her face held such sorrow. How could I cope with that, with Susan haunting me?'

'You believe that she's haunting you?'

'They all do. They turn up in the night or when no-one else is around and they just stand there. Sometimes they shout and curse me and tell me they're waiting for me. I beg them to go away but they never listen. In the end I knew what I had to do. I have to join them, to suffer like they did. I have to earn their forgiveness...'

The screen went blank.

'I don't think he ate again voluntarily after that interview.' Mason mused. 'What you see now is a result of the following four months of self neglect.' All eyes turned to John who remained unmoved. The saliva that strung from his mouth glistened in the spotlight.

'Susan Holland had suffered a catastrophic stroke in her sleep at the age of twenty four and she was, as I said earlier, the last case that John worked on before his collapse. Since he didn't have the time or the inclination to hide the case records we do have the tapes available, but I warn you, it's not easy listening.'

A low hiss filled the theatre. There was a muffled click.

'The date is February sixth two thousand and four. It is twelve thirty five in the afternoon and I am Doctor John Dante, presiding over the post mortem examination of Miss Susan Holland, a female Caucasian in her early twenties who was pronounced dead this morning from unknown causes. The initial visual assessment gives no firm indication and there are no signs of impact, ligature or penetrative wounding. There is no exceptional discolouration or staining of the skin and no inflammation.'

In the background a metallic rattle suggested a wheeled trolley replete with tools.

'I'm about to commence the visceral examination making my first entry at the subjects left collarbone.'

'No.' It was the faintest of voices, but recognisably female.

'I... er... I'll gain access to the...'

'No! What are you doing? I don't want to die. Please!' The scream that followed obliterated any other sounds. The recording crackled as the noise compressed and distorted the speakers with overload. The cry ended abruptly, choked off in a muffled gargle.

'The longitudinal incision will... oh god! You've got to keep still! I can't work if you won't keep still!' More screams pierced the auditorium, some stifled as if she were screaming down her nose. 'It'll be over soon, I promise. Please be quiet. If anyone hears you I'm done for. Please, I'm so sorry.' There were rattles and bangs that suggested a monumental struggle and the sound of metal hitting a hard floor, and still the screams of protest went on, perforated with choked whimpers and pleading.

'... Peeling aside the skin to expose the sternum,' A high shriek tore through the room followed by spasmodic coughing and then a sigh; the kind of sigh that empties a body of everything. 'There are no signs of peritoneal attachment or lung infection, and the myofascia appears to be... to be...' There was a pause followed by the harsh clatter of steel and the slow and rhythmic sobbing of a man destroyed.

Click!

There was silence in the theatre. One man moved out of his seat to sit in the aisle with his head between his knees as Mason strode out to centre stage.

'We've come to that part of the proceedings where I ask for questions...' several hands shot into the air, 'but since the first one is so obvious I'll take the liberty of asking it myself.' Mason continued. The hands went down again. 'Why, if Susan Holland is dead, can we hear her voice on the recording? Well, according to the boffins in the university audio visual department, John is the source of both voices. Absurd as it may seem, if we distance ourselves emotionally from the content of the recording and analyse it as merely a collection of sounds it becomes apparent, with the use of the right equipment, that the voices never actually overlap. Although I have to admit, it is pretty convincing. John is of course completely unaware that he's playing both roles.'

A hand went up at the back of the room. Mason nodded in acknowledgement.

'I've no wish to appear cynical sir,' a tall student with an Indian accent stood up to speak, 'but it seems to me that a great deal of effort has been spent to discredit the patients account and absolutely none at all to gather any evidence that doctor Dante may actually have been telling the truth. Is it possible that we are guilty of making the facts fit our expectation of them?' Mason appeared momentarily shocked that someone could so unsubtly accuse him of having a blinkered scientific approach.

'Yes of course it is,' Mason shrugged, 'and having known John in the past I would rather believe him to be delusional than have to admit to the only possible alternative, but it's a matter of behavioural context. What you see here before you', he gestured toward John, 'is the result of the burden of guilt. Any man who is truly capable of the acts that John claims to have committed would not have felt the guilt that John felt and would therefore probably be still at large. I'm not saying that John's account of events cannot be possible. What I'm saying is that the guilt he exhibits is the one major piece of behavioural evidence that serves to undermine his delusion. That is why I find it inconceivable that John is the murderer that he claims to be. Now, are there any other questions?'

'What's your prognosis?' A small voice asked from three rows back.

'John's condition is terminal.' Mason murmured, walking back to his lectern. He pressed a few keys and an electroencephalograph trace appeared on the screen. 'The EEG trace that you're seeing is being taken as we speak. If you look in your notes you'll see a similar trace taken two weeks ago. I'd estimate the drop in signal amplitude to be approximately twelve percent over that period. What this means is that the electrical activity in John's brain is slowly dying away. If he continues to attenuate at this rate I'd say that he's got about three weeks, maybe a month, but the one saving grace is that he won't know that it's happening.' He moved back to centre stage. 'Ladies and gentlemen, I'll be the first to admit that I've made mistakes in the handling of John's case. We are all human and I'm sure that you will make your own mistakes as your careers progress, but these things are forgivable in most cases. The important thing is that we learn from them.'

A dull buzzing noise filled the room.

'And thus the mighty dinner bell brings us soundly down to earth.' Mason smiled. 'Take your notes with you and make sure that you read through them. There's a lot to take in.'

As the students filed out of the lecture theatre Mason knew that some of them would end up knowing far more than he did. That was the nature of progress. But however much they knew, within the complete span of human behaviour it would still amount to nothing at all.

***

Mister Thompson pushed John's chair slowly along the stark, off white hospital corridor.

'Did you hear that John?' Susan Holland hissed into his ear as one of the large wheels ran over her trailing gut. 'It won't be long now.'

*****

Kirlia.

Carlos chuntered a few expletives under his breath and then threw the dregs of his vodka to the back of his throat. He hunched over his laptop in the dimness of his home office, his round face a pallid glow in the screen light.

He had writers block. He'd been sitting there for the past two hours faced with the end of all nightmares for a middle aged man in his profession; a blank document. Getting drunk usually helped. It encouraged his dark side. But not today.

He stood up. His stiffened neck muscles tore as he moved. He found the vodka bottle and poured himself another measure or two of liquid inspiration.

His eyes were dry and tired, which didn't help. He wore contact lenses; had done for years. He'd started with the hard plastic ones and never had a single problem with them. You could clean them with washing up liquid, bleach them, whatever you wanted. Just give them a good rinse and you were off.

His optician had recommended that he change to a different material. Something to do with gas transfer apparently. Bollocks! New stuff comes in, old stuff goes out. That's the way it is. Which one was he, he wondered.

The new lenses had been a pain in the arse since day one. They grabbed at his eyes like fucking blu-tac. He wanted to go back to his old ones but after a two week trial period waiting for his eyes to 'adjust' to the new ones, he found that he couldn't tolerate them anymore.

The jelly ones also cost a bloody small fortune and if his writer's block continued he wouldn't be able to afford them anyway.

He sat at his desk hoping that a few more minutes of mental distraction might help him crawl out of his stagnation. He launched his internet browser and typed 'contact lens suppliers' into the search bar.

Google did its thing and presented him with the first ten of nine hundred and sixty six thousand listings. He grunted to himself. You'd think that with all their cash and brain power, they'd be able to narrow it down a bit fucking more than this.

He tried the top six or seven links. The prices were so similar it was as if they all knew each other. He could practically hear them all bloody sniggering in the background.

He moved on a few pages and picked one at random, kirlia.co.ua. Somewhere in Eastern Europe by the look of the address suffix.

The screen went blank for half a second and then filled with several small pictures surrounded by Cyrillic text. He copied a few chunks into an online translator. It was all the usual claptrap about 'special coatings' and 'you to see in sharp clearness what is the real'. Not worth the effort. He trawled down through the page until he got to the price list. He was pleasantly surprised. They were less than half of what he currently paid, including shipping, and let's face it, the vodka told him, so long as he entered the prescription correctly a lens is a lens, right?

He took the risk, filling in the dialogue boxes from the details on his current lens package as best he could and ticking all of the check boxes. He made his payment, which was courteously accepted, and then sat back feeling happy at having stuck it to the man.

Remarkably, his consignment arrived only eight days later. Now that's fucking service, he thought to himself. That's what happens when you pick a company that actually wants to do business.

As luck would have it his current lenses were the two weekly variety and were about due for the dung pile. He pulled open the packaging as he mounted the stairs heading for the bathroom mirror.

The manufacturers had even seen fit to include a small bottle of rinsing fluid. No extras. He liked that.

He fumbled about with the individual foil sealed containers and, after carefully rinsing each lens, he popped them in.

'Wow!' He exclaimed aloud. Talk about comfort. He really couldn't feel them at all, and as for clarity, it was like watching HDTV for the first time. He stared around him, hardly daring to blink in case it all went pear shaped. Everything that he looked at had a real hard edge to it. Even the smallest and most distant objects seemed to stand alone, with every line diamond sharp, almost sparkling.

Carlos smiled to himself as he left the house.

He had a meeting with his publisher that morning and things always went the same way. He turned up on the dot, and she didn't. He'd brought a sandwich with him to pass the time, and anyway it would give him a chance to chat up that receptionist of hers. The blonde one with the nice arse.

He strolled into the reception area noticing details around him that he'd never even known were there before. The receptionist greeted him with her usual fixed and pearly smile.

'What can we do for you today Mr. Soames?' She asked cheerfully.

'A cup of strong coffee wouldn't go amiss gorgeous.' Carlos replied quickly. 'I'm here to see Claris.'

Her face didn't change, but something did. It seemed to Carlos that maybe a light had gone out further along the corridor. The place just suddenly darkened. She turned away from him.

Carlos shrugged lightly to himself and then wandered off in search of somewhere to sit. Even the chairs looked different, newer somehow. They had a kind of brightness to them. He sat down in a random seat and pulled a plastic sandwich bag from his jacket pocket. He looked around him for something to read. As he scanned the reception desk a light came on from somewhere behind the divider. It was bright, multicoloured and cloud like. As soon as it came, it vanished. Then the telephone rang. Each time the phone chimed, the lights came back, dancing over it in flashing hues, in time with the ring tone.

The receptionist rushed to answer it with Carlos' coffee in her hand and then patched the call through before replacing the receiver.

'God.' Carlos commented. 'That must get right on your tits after a while.'

'What?' The receptionist answered, gathering up the coffee cup.

'That bloody phone.' Carlos answered. 'Specially designed for deaf people is it?' He almost slapped himself across the face. What the hell would a deaf person need a telephone for? The receptionist gave him a quizzical glance before walking around with his coffee. She put it onto the small table in front of him.

He watched her bend over, trying not to look as if he was staring in at her cleavage. He nodded his gratitude and she turned to leave. This was the best part, Carlos drooled inwardly. God, that arse was a fucking work of art. He watched her buttocks sway back and forth but found himself being distracted by something in her lower back as she walked. There was a kind of otherworldly glow about it, as if she were being lit up from within. He looked harder, forcing his eyes to dissect the image.

There really was something else there. A small iridescence that moved inside of her. His focus sharpened and he could make out lines in the light. The lines defined a tiny foetal silhouette.

He blinked hard and the image faltered. He should have been amazed but the only thing that occurred to him was that some bastard had knocked her up before he'd had a chance to get in there.

His head began to ache and he felt a little dizzy. Maybe these lenses needed some getting used to after all. If Claris didn't show up soon he'd go home. Five minutes later she arrived but Carlos was too distracted by now to offer anything productive. They decided to postpone for a few days.

Carlos walked out of the office. The receptionist, who was on the phone, gave him a tired smile.

'Congratulations by the way.' Carlos called out.

'What?' She answered, almost dropping the receiver.

'The baby.' Carlos smiled. 'When's it due?'

'You can tell?' She whispered, standing up and holding her stomach in. 'Already?'

'Let's call it a knack.' Carlos replied. 'My dad was a gynaecologist. He used to work weekends 'cos he liked to keep his hand in!'

His quip fell on stony ground. He walked out. Some people have got no sense of fucking humour.

As he stepped onto the pavement it was like walking into a circus tent. Everything glowed brighter than daylight. If he didn't know better he'd suspect that someone had spiked his coffee. The last time he'd seen anything like this was in nineteen eighty eight when he and his girlfriend had shared an experimental trip. The walls of his room had moved with him as he breathed and he'd spent several hours in bed with her, planting soft paisley kisses on her breasts.

It was like that now, but without the warm groovy feeling inside.

Some kids ran past him. Probably playing truant from school. To anyone else they looked like a team of young muggers, but to Carlos' new eyes they rolled along the ground like tumbling jewels, glittering with life. He could barely take his eyes off them.

Is that what he was seeing? He asked himself. Life?

There was an old lady across the street, hoisting a Zimmer frame ahead of her and then hobbling to catch up. Her light was muddy, dim and weak. He glanced at her knees, two dark caverns in the barely visible pool of silver grey. She was probably arthritic. Maybe even had plastic knees.

Yes. That's what it was, he told himself. He could see Life.

Once home he fired up his laptop and went straight back to the website. He printed the entire content to a .pdf file and then attached it to an email.

It had been a long time since he'd spoken to Yulia. She was his ex-wife's best friend and had taken her side during their acrimonious divorce. But that was all water under the bridge. Let bygones be bygones he told himself. Especially since she was the only person he knew who may be able to translate all this crap. He still had her email address, and that of his ex-wife, and yet he'd never paused to ponder the significance of this.

He loaded the email with some bullshit about doing research for a product comparison article and would she please, please do him a favour and give him the English version. He'd be ever so grateful, honest.

He pushed the send button.

He spent the next few hours writing down what had happened during the day because you never know when you're going to need good copy.

He made himself a nightcap and then went to bed. He laid in the darkness, staring at the shadowed ceiling. The new lenses were out now but it was as if there was some persistence of vision effect. He swore that he could still see shimmering lights floating around him.

The following morning he wore the lenses again, and again he saw the world anew.

It was supermarket day, and being a family of one he didn't need a shopping list. He always bought the same things and he only went there because it was cheaper than the corner shop.

His favourite part of the trip was the pub lunch on the way there. He pushed open the pub door and strolled inside. Frank, the landlord, greeted him with a smile.

'Same as usual Carlos?' He asked, already punching into the cash register.

'Nothing but the best Frankie.' Carlos replied taking a stool by the bar. He looked around the room. The place was packed by its usual standards. Two young Goths sharing a pint of lager in one corner and a strange looking old bloke sitting alone by the window. He didn't even have a drink. He just sat there in old dusty clothing, his dark sunken eyes staring into nowhere. He looked like someone had killed him and dumped his body there. He gave Carlos the creeps.

'Halloween's a bit fucking early eh!' He sniggered, leaning toward the barman. The two Goths immediately finished up their shared drink and walked out, shooting a dirty look at Carlos on the way.

'Thanks for that.' Frank muttered.

'I didn't mean them.' Carlos replied, turning to look at the old man by the window. 'I meant...'

There was no-one there.

Carlos sighed deeply and then hopped off the stool bound for the toilet. The usual smell of old piss and pine cubes assailed his senses as he entered. He took his place at one of the urinals. When he'd finished he turned to the basin to wash his hands. The old man was standing in the corner, again staring at nothing.

'Thanks for letting me take the rap for that mate.' Carlos grunted, wiping his damp hands on a paper towel. The man didn't even seem to acknowledge his presence. Carlos pulled open the door and walked out into the bar.

He looked over by the window. The old man was sitting there.

'This some kind of joke is it?' Carlos shouted to Frank. 'The fucking zombie twins!'

Frank just shrugged. 'Maybe I'll just skip lunch today then eh?' Carlos grunted, walking out of the pub. Frank watched him go, shook his head dejectedly and unfolded the racing pages.

Carlos felt disinclined to do anything much now that his routine had been so thoroughly disrupted but he needed to fill the cupboards and so he continued on.

The supermarket was like the loser's club trip. Not a single smiling face. Carlos felt dirty just breathing the same air as these jobless nobodies. Wave upon wave of lager laden sweaty piss heads and thirteen year old mothers with plastic pushchairs and snotty toddlers, piling their trolleys with disposable nappies and rash cream. None of them had a life and they were too stupid to want one. Give any of them satellite TV and twenty ciggies and they were yours forever.

Not like that woman over there in the wheelchair. He watched her being pushed slowly along the aisle. She had some kind of breathing apparatus on her face. There were gas bottles mounted behind the chair. Poor cow, Carlos thought. Not sure about the funny hat though. He walked a little closer to her for a better look. Bloody weird hat she was wearing. He was about to laugh inwardly, when it moved.

His vision seemed to zoom forward of its own volition. He felt dizzy with the speed of it. The thing on her head was slug like, but scaly and wet. It had stubby, three fingered claws that dug into each side of her face and a thick dark proboscis that it inserted through the crown of her head. It had a long tail that wrapped tightly around her pale thin neck, and it was feeding from her.

It was sucking the energy straight out of her, drinking her life force and bleeding her dry. And as if that wasn't enough, it had some kind of pulsating tube pushed deep into her lungs from behind, through which it excreted oily black shit.

And no·one else could see it.

Carlos stared, open mouthed as it flicked the air with stunted useless leathery wings.

'You want a fucking photo mate?' Her helper's voice grunted angrily.

'What?' Carlos gasped. 'Oh, no, sorry.' He turned away and walked quickly for the exit, barely suppressing the urge to lift his hand to his mouth.

He half walked, half jogged home. No simple task for a man of his size. He barged inside the house and then stood breathless with his back to the door. His wall mounted telephone was flashing the fact that he had one new message. He picked up the receiver and poked at the buttons.

Yulia's voice spoke to him. Her guttural Russian accent grated on him like an embarrassing memory.

'Typical Carlos. Only bloddy calling when you wanting something. Can't believe you actually try this thing. Am halfway through translating. I put in email this part. You know what these are, yes? Special, for seeing the ghosts. You must be bloddy madman!' The phone went dead.

He played the message again, and then a third time, just to make sure he'd heard it right.

The lenses were made especially for seeing ghosts. That's what Yulia had said, no matter how much he tried to re·hear it in his mind.

He lurched to his laptop and jabbed the power button. He tapped his fingers impatiently on the desk top while he waited for it to boot.

For seeing ghosts, he repeated in his mind. Is that even possible? Surely not.

He went straight to the email application and pulled down Yulia's message. He opened the attachment and started reading.

It began with a brief history of Kirlian photography. Carlos made notes to Google with. Apparently this Kirlian bloke had discovered a means by which to photograph the electromagnetic corona produced by living organisms. By coating photographic film and applying various voltages he captured images of what he believed to be the human aura. By refining the coating compound he was able to narrow down the field frequency.

That was in the late nineteen sixties, and things had progressed considerably since then. Another mad professor, Andre Maslik, had taken up where Kirlian left off and developed special lens coatings that could react to very subtle and exceptionally high frequencies...

'It isn't the lenses.' Carlos whispered to himself. 'It's the bloody soaking solution.'

And this wasn't a product... It was a field trial.

He'd signed up for a fucking field trial.

He scrolled down to the 'directions for use' section. He read a few lines. His heart nearly dropped out of his arse. How could he have been so fucking stupid?

The lenses were just a delivery system designed to hold the fluid against the cornea until it had time to... penetrate. 'What does that mean?' Carlos muttered, his mind denying the obvious.

'Dosage, dosage...' He chanted, scanning the document further until he found it.

'One drop in each lens, then no more for six weeks, after which a further drop may be administered if required... '

He'd thought it was rinsing solution. No wonder the bottle was so small. He'd put four drops in each lens for two consecutive days! Did that matter?

'Of course it does! Silly bastard!' Carlos shouted at himself.

He opened his browser again and typed 'Andre Maslik' into the search bar. Google returned perhaps ten links, one of which was a news item issued in Ukraine. He flicked to the page and block copied everything into an online translator. He scanned the resulting text.

Andre Maslik was dead. He'd been discovered in his bathroom only three days ago. Police were viewing the circumstances as suspicious. There was a small picture. Carlos gasped.

It was the zombie twins from the pub.

Carlos flicked back to the Google listing.

Last on the list was a forum showing several recent references to Andre Maslik. Carlos clicked the link and searched through the latest posts. Again he block copied everything he found into the translator.

The last few entries almost took his breath:

'Is it true, what they are saying in the news, that Andre is dead?'

'Yes, I believe so.'

'And is it also true, what the others are saying. That when he was found, his eyes were missing?'

'This has not been confirmed.'

'And that they were later discovered in his stomach?'

There were no further entries. The final one had been posted yesterday evening.

44

Carlos sat back in his chair. He wondered if there were others out there like him, tasting the sourness of rising panic in their throats, not knowing what to do next.

His eyes were found in his stomach, Carlos reminded himself. How can that happen?

He needed to hide. And where better than the vodka bottle? It had never failed him in the past.

He stood up and walked toward the kitchen. He pushed open the door and then fell back. Standing in the kitchen was Andre Maslik. His skin dust white and flaking. Where his eyes should have been were dry and blackened voids. His purple mouth was locked in the endless repetition of words that Carlos could neither hear nor read. Andre walked towards him.

Carlos staggered backward, sick with fear. He backed into his desk which rocked violently. His printer sprang to life churning out page after page of text:

Do not see....
Do not see....
Do not see....
Do not see....
Do not see....
Do not see....

...

The screen of his laptop followed suit, flashing endless lines of white on black.

'Alright! Alright!' Carlos screamed, raising an arm to his face, panic cracking his voice. 'I get the fucking message!'

The printer stopped. Andre was gone.

Carlos panted heavily. He was about ten seconds from a heart attack.

He gathered his thoughts as best he could and set off up the stairs. He headed straight for the bathroom mirror and with trembling fingers, and taking several attempts, he pinched out his lenses. In the medicine cabinet was a large bottle of his old lens rinsing solution. He popped the cap, opened his eyes and squirted his eyeballs as vigorously as he dared. He didn't stop until the bottle was empty.

He rolled his eyes and blinked hard, silently praying that this was enough to undo the damage.

He washed his face, relaxing a little under the distraction of the cool water.

He patted his face dry with a towel and walked into his bedroom.

His old glasses were the cheapest available on the opticians cut price rack. He'd been pressured into buying them as a backup when he bought his old contacts. He had to rummage about in the dark recesses of his bedside drawer to dig them out.

At minus five dioptres the lenses were heavy and thick and they made his eyes look two feet further away than the rest of his face. The frames were square and made of black wire. The weight of them always made his nose ache.

He put them on, grimacing in the knowledge that he now looked like a bloody child molester.

He walked slowly down the stairs to the living room. He knew as soon as he began to push the door open that there was something in there. Breathing deeply, Carlos looked around the door.

Andre was standing in the middle of the room but this time he'd seen fit to invite a few friends. A young woman wearing a flowery dress, sores weeping on her grey face, shuffled toward him in silence. Behind her a young man, the whiteness of bone protruding viciously from one side of his broken neck and rope marks tracing a reddened path up his face. There were others also, as yet out of focus, but all coming for him and all mouthing endlessly, 'Do not see...'

Carlos did the sensible thing. He turned and fled.

'The hospital.' Carlos gasped to himself as he ran down the street. Surely they'd have something to wash this stuff out of his eyes, and it was only about a mile away.

It was little short of torture, asking his overweight, middle aged, couch potato body to carry him an entire mile without stopping for a pint and a pie. His chest heaved and his legs burned. His glasses, cold in the night air, condensed his sweat, making it impossible to see. But he didn't stop. Not once. Until he found an entrance to the hospital grounds.

The casualty department was on the other side of the complex but he needed to be near other people so he decided to walk through the building.

Not knowing his way around he drifted into the nearest corridor. There were several wards branching off to each side. He glanced sideways into a set of double doors, hoping to see a member of staff who could give him directions.

There was a bed in a side room. The woman lying in it looked skeletal. Her arm rested on top of the bedclothes, the skin hung from it in a baggy flap. You didn't need a PhD to know that she hadn't long left. Her family were standing around the bed, waiting in silence.

One of them moved aside slightly and Carlos caught a glimpse of something. He stepped closer to the door. The people in the room were too preoccupied to notice him.

It was another one of those slug things. Like the one in the supermarket, but more developed. This one had bigger wings, and eyes. White, moist, weeping eyes that rolled in loose sockets either side of it's bulbous head. It sat hunched on her belly, it's proboscis pushed deep into her vagina and it's rectum piercing her liver.

Carlos shrank back. He walked further into the ward, looking desperately for someone to help him.

They all had them.

47

Every single patient had one of these disgusting creatures attached in one way or another. One man had a small one, a young one Carlos guessed, hanging from his face.

They were some kind of ethereal parasite, leeching unseen and unfelt from their victims. Growing ever stronger on the life energy of people that didn't even know they were there. Their hosts merely suffered, and died.

Carlos walked over to a man who had one of the parasites hanging from his back. It fed from his throat, excreting into his stomach. Carlos looked closely at it. He leaned toward it and looked into its pearly white eye.

It saw him. And it was afraid.

In a frenzy of flapping leathery wings it withdrew its proboscis from its host's throat and set it high in the air. The man began to choke and convulse. Carlos looked around him as the other creatures did the same, each one curling back and holding it's damp bristled feeding tube erect, and each host falling one by one into convulsion. Suddenly there were hospital staff everywhere as the whole ward devolved into chaos.

Carlos simply stared. What were they doing? Then he realised.

They were calling out. God alone knew what sound they would be making if he'd had the ears to hear them.

An unseen darkness descended on the room. A black light that only he could see. The creatures before him were merely larvae. Foetal masses that used human souls as placenta. Foul infants whose only defence was their invisibility.

The black light became brighter, if such a thing were possible, and Carlos knew then that something terrible was coming and that its only purpose was to defend its children.

'Do not see...'

Carlos ran out of the ward and down the corridor. He knew now that Andre had actually been trying to warn him. Some things just don't want to be seen, so keep your fat fucking nose out! Why hadn't he written that on the sodding printer?

He ran into the nearest toilet cubicle and locked the door. He sat down on the pedestal with his head in his hands. What the hell was he doing? Whatever was coming after him inhabited an entirely different spectrum! It was probably completely unaware of the hospital building and more than capable of passing through its thick stone walls like piss through a sieve.

As the first teardrops formed on Carlos' eyelids the black light found him.

So intense was it that even the harsh brightness of the toilet cubicle light was cancelled out in Carlos' stricken consciousness.

There was an angel in the light. Terrifying in its dark brilliance it hovered above him as he cowered. Huge and graceful its glistening wings seemed to devour everything that they touched. Its face was almost bland in its calmness, almost human in its beauty.

It occurred to Carlos that if this was what those slugs grew up to be, then maybe it was worth a few souls.

The dark creature regarded him closely, searching him, but for what?

For weakness. Carlos knew then that he could run, but he couldn't hide. This was a breeder.

The angel writhed and squirmed, bringing forth a long ovipositor with which it probed him. Carlos felt nothing. The sharp tube danced around his body, back and forth, up and down...

Eenie... Meenie... Miney...

The tube struck violently into his chest. Carlos felt a crippling cold that crushed his heart like a steel fist. He couldn't breathe. He could barely move.

49

A stillborn scream left his throat. No-one would hear it.

'Do not see...' A voice in his mind insisted. 'Do not see...'

Carlos threw off his glasses. He lifted his hands to his eyes, and screaming again, he drew his fingernails across them.

***

'He's had a massive heart attack Mrs Soames.' The doctor told her. 'He's fortunate to be alive actually.'

'I'm not Mrs Soames any more.' Erica replied. 'We're divorced, but I'm all the family he has.'

She watched him solemnly as he lay sedated in the hospital bed. Irritating machines emitted smug bleeps from one corner of the room.

'What happened to his eyes?' She asked.

'No idea.' The doctor replied. 'But the damage is fairly substantial. He'll need corneal transplants if he's going to see again. Luckily we've had quite a few donations recently... From eastern Europe.'

*****

How do you like yours?

'My name is Julia Smedly. Well, it's not my real name obviously, but then I'm getting a little ahead of myself. Let me begin by asking you a few questions.

How do you like your potatoes? Mashed? Boiled? Chipped and fried perhaps?

What about your ideal car? Is it curved and sporty or boxy and reliable?

Do you prefer a holiday in the African sun, or skiing in the Pyrenees?

In the end does it really matter? It'd be a poor state of affairs if we all liked the same things.

What about sex then? Do you like yours with a man or a woman? Both perhaps? Or God forbid, with animals, minerals or vegetables?

The point I'm making is that no-one can help the way they feel; the way that they're designed. It's all a part of nature's limitless abundance and rich variety. We can of course, depending on the strength of our urges and the opposing force of our moral convictions, choose whether or not to act upon those feelings. But we cannot help having them.

As the world of human endeavour broadens, the scope of our sexuality is never far behind, although it can't be compared to how it was say, two thousand years ago when the Romans were in charge. They really knew how to throw a party! Then the emergence of Christianity brought us headlong into the sexual dark ages, choking off any possibility of the use of sex as a recreational activity, and you couldn't have a good hard shag all through the middle ages unless you were prepared to accept that an omniscient father figure was sitting at the bottom of the bed watching your arse bobbing up and down and that he could give it a good hard slap if you looked as if you were enjoying it too much.

The Victorians? Don't even get me started. Numb from the waist down!

Then at last the swinging sixties. No risk of pregnancy, a pill to cure all known venereal disease and plenty of willing sexual scientists to experiment with. Thus the field of human eroticism grows ever wider.

Some things though, will never be accepted.

Despite the fact that certain 'practices' have always been with us, flitting through the tempting velvet darkness that lies beyond the horizons of sexual normalcy they are, although generally quite harmless, regarded with great distaste.

Yes, I'm normal in virtually every respect. I'm a young and healthy female. I've had a good upbringing, enjoying the attention of loving parents. I have several siblings who have beautiful families of their own. I'm heterosexual, as if that matters at all, and I go for the standard male characteristics. I like a tall, firmly set man of approximately my age with a full head of thick hair; dark and wavy preferably. I like good musculature and straight white teeth and I'm a sucker for the strong, silent type. So you see I really am quite normal... apart from the fact that they also have to be dead.

I mean, it's not like they're in short supply is it? Just hard to actually meet, that's the problem. That's why I worked as a mortician, to improve my romantic opportunities. But I'm leaping ahead again.

I was fifteen when I realised my predilection for 'post mortem relationships' as I call them. An interest in the opposite sex had kicked off in the usual way and at the right age. There was the girlish giggling between friends as the boys walked past in the school corridors and the secret exploratory fumbling when the lights went out at the extra curricular drama club. I did my fair share of kissing, but no tongues please, and of course I became aroused. But in retrospect, glorious as these sensations were, they were nothing compared to what happened the day that I discovered my true self.

Kevin Washby – corpse number three. That's what it said on the program, I've still got it stashed away with other mementos in my bedroom drawer. As I said, I was a member of the school drama club and we were putting on a pantomime loosely based on Robinson Crusoe except that it had Dracula in it and the Easter bunny. I was in the chorus.

We had this scene where Count Dracula had just finished off three peasants to the tune of 'food glorious food' when I saw him, Kevin that is, lying on the stage motionless with his throat raised and lashings of fake blood soaked into his ragged clothes.

It was like being kissed between my legs; a sort of hot fluttering. I'm no poet and I've yet to read a poem that adequately describes what it's like to be turned on like a firework display on New Years Eve, but I think you know what I'm talking about. It was maybe an hour later that I finally got to be alone. I ran to the girls toilets and sat in a cubicle in darkness with my hands down my panties. After five minutes of frenzied finger action I threw a massive, bone shaking gusher of an orgasm. Honestly, I almost fell off the fucking pot! When I got home I must have masturbated almost continuously for the rest of the night. The image just kept coming back at me for days after.

John Vault

I didn't fully realise at first what it was that had sent me over the top. I thought that maybe I just fancied Kevin Washby so I made a point of chatting him up over the next few weeks and when I did finally get to give him a good snogging I realised that I'd made a mistake. Oh it was okay, don't get me wrong, but it wasn't until I saw him in my minds eye, cold and immobile, that my loins freaked.

That's how it was for a few years until university. I fell in with a group of Goths, probably because most of them looked like they were dead, but you can't fool yourself. I needed the real thing. When I left uni I went to work for a local funeral director. I was twenty four when true love finally came along.

Alex Dawson, that was his name, I have a picture of the two of us together, would you like to see it? Well, perhaps not.

Anyway, I went into work one day and there he was; my soul mate. My perfect man. God he was seriously lush, dead as a doornail and not a mark on him. It was love at first sight, not that I'm into all that romantic slush, but he loved me too, I could tell.

He was the son of a local councillor and aspiring commons backbencher. He was well educated and witty. We never argued. We just fitted together. We had deep and meaningful conversations about every conceivable subject and we wanted to be together forever.

It would have been nice, just him and me, in a timeless bubble of love with nothing but sex and chocolate. But it can't ever be that way. I'm not stupid. I know I have to deal with the real world. Sooner or later his family would want him back. We spent a couple of hours in tearful torment until we made our decision to elope.

The night before Alex's funeral I sneaked in through the back door of the funeral parlour. I'd already managed to get a key cut earlier that day. Alex was there in the semi-darkness waiting for me

54

just like we'd agreed. He'd never let me down. We were in love.

We both knew that he couldn't sit in the front seat of the hearse; he had to hide in the back. It all went so smoothly until the alarms went off. Apparently there were two alarm systems, one for the main building and one for the garage. We tripped the garage alarm so we had to leave quickly before the police arrived. We sped off into the night, screaming and giggling.

We must have driven for about an hour, completely absorbed in the rush. I eventually pulled over into some trees and breathed a deep sigh of relief. I clambered into the back of the hearse and we lay together in silence for a while trying to take in the enormity of what we'd done. Like I said, I'm no romantic but even I know when the time is right.

There was no fumbling or clumsiness despite the lack of room. It was a lingering kiss followed by slow deliberation. Once we were both naked I climbed aboard and straddled him. It was all so easy, like it was meant to be. I was getting into rhythm, pushing slowly back and forth, working us both up into a lather. That's when the back doors suddenly flew open and half a dozen police officers stared in on us, picking out our nakedness with torchlight.

Our love was doomed from then on. Alex's parents refused to let us see each other, (although for some reason they managed to avoid any further involvement from the police), and I was fired from my job.

I hit a little depression for a few months. Heart broken I suppose. Anyway the long and the short of it is that I decided that from then on I'd never waste time again. Why should love wait? If it's right, it's right.

A year or so later I met James. I'd gone to a nightclub with friends and we accidentally bumped asses on the dance floor. Yes, yes I know what you're

thinking, what happened to the dead guy thing?
Well I'm coming to that. So James and I, we really
hit it off. After a couple of months we were
inseparable. He was something of a gentleman and
it took a little while before we got 'down and dirty' if
you get my drift.

In the end, (I had to push him a little) he finally
admitted that he loved me and that he wanted me to
love him. I tried to explain to him that each time I
thought that I'd found true love the relationship had
turned out to be somewhat short lived. He seemed
confident that our love would be different and that
we shouldn't wait to be together forever.

I hardly have to tell you that this was just music to
my ears. We were the same, James and I. We had an
understanding.

I wanted to make our first time special so one day,
when I knew he was at work, I went to his flat. I
pushed back the furniture and made the living room
a little cosier by putting coloured veils over the
lamps. I put scented candles in each corner and then
hit the kitchen to make my special spaghetti
Bolognese.

James arrived home a little late. This was good
because I had to put together a few finishing touches.
Let's just say he looked a little surprised when he
did turn up. I ran him a nice hot bath.

We had a cosy candle lit meal and then we were at
it. It started out soft but then turned rapid fire, you
know, all mouth and trousers. I have to say that
James was an impressive lover. He was either very
experienced or extremely talented. He must have
had the constitution of a horse because it took
perhaps an hour before the Valium kicked in. He
went off to sleep, dozing in the musky scents of
sexual aftermath. I waited quietly; the tension
crowding into my loins and making me ache.

Twenty minutes I waited before I put the plastic bag over his head and pulled it tight. Then it was my turn to rattle his bones.

It's been about two months now and the dim lighting and scented candles are still working a treat. James was right. We are meant to be together.

Why should love wait?'

*****

A brief moment of lucidity.

Daniel was standing on an old stone bridge. A wide
viaduct, built in the days when men knew how to
work stone. Long since closed to traffic due to its age,
it was still used as a thoroughfare for people who
moved across the valley between home and town on
foot. At it's highest it cleared the meandering stream
below by over eighty feet. It was lined on each side
with walls that were two and a half feet thick and
five feet high, topped with huge rough cut coping
stones. At thirteen he'd ridden his bicycle all the
way along, almost a kilometre, on top of one of those
walls for a dare. The bridge was so exposed that it
caught some fairly severe and random cross winds
and if he'd been blown over the edge to his death he
certainly wouldn't have been the first. It had been
possibly the most terrifying experience of his life and
even now, at almost sixteen years old his gut
rebelled at the thought of even standing on one of
those walls.

Yet here he was.

He stood with the toes of his trainers barely in line
with the outer edge of the wall. There were rusty
and decrepit gas lamp posts set at regular intervals
along the bridge. He was holding onto the one
immediately to his left with an outstretched arm
and peering down into the abyss. The night was
dark but the full of the moon cast a jagged silver line

onto the still blackness of the dam that had been diverted from the stream for use by the local fishing club. It wasn't particularly deep. Certainly not deep enough to save him from a fall of this height.

A sudden gust of wind unnerved him enough to make him step back slightly. When it subsided he shuffled forward again, ever closer to the edge.

He was waiting for someone. Someone that he remembered arranging this absurd rendezvous with but couldn't actually bring to mind. Why the hell would he possibly have arranged something like this?

His nerves settled down a little, having become more accustomed to his surroundings. He resolved to wait a little longer, a few more minutes perhaps, and then if whoever it was didn't show up he'd go home. He gripped the gas lamp a little tighter in an effort to reassure himself that it was still there.

A pale grey cloud skipped quickly across the face of the moon. Daniel watched the surface of the dam darken. It was then that he heard the sound of a gentle cough behind him.

It was then that he remembered...

It was a school day. Mondays were always a bitch because at fifteen years old Daniel wasn't big on waking up in the morning, especially when he'd spent a late night hanging around the back of the offy with his mates and several bottles of cider.

His mother screamed his name from downstairs for maybe the sixth time. The pitch of her voice was bordering on ultrasound. He threw back the duvet and swung his legs over the edge of the bed. He stood up, yawned, dipped his hand into his undies to scratch his nuts and then ambled toward the bathroom. His younger sister Trina had already commandeered the sink, which pissed him off. She was leaning into the bathroom mirror, brushing her teeth, wearing only panties and a training bra. She spotted him in the mirror as he approached. She turned and slammed the door shut in his face.

He woke up again.

'Bloody hell!' He gasped, having realised that he'd just dreamt the last two or three minutes. His mother screamed his name from downstairs. He rolled out of bed, washed, dressed and headed down for breakfast, squeezing himself in at the table and grabbing a slice of toast. Trina was in the kitchen complaining that there never seemed to be a clean bowl available because Daniel was too lazy to wash up. He ignored her as he always did. He started to tell his dad about his weird dream when Trina cut her finger on a knife at the bottom of the sink. She shrieked and leapt back, knocking the draining board with her elbow. Half a dozen plates shattered on the kitchen floor.

Daniel woke up again.

He couldn't quite believe it this time. His heart thumped loudly and cold sweat stood out on his brow. His mother screamed his name from downstairs...

The bus queue was that in name only. As soon as the old school double decker rounded the corner and came into view all hell broke loose amongst the twenty or so children who had been waiting for the last fifteen minutes in the pouring rain. The concrete bus shelter had been badly vandalised so often that the council had refused to replace it. The doors folded back with a loud hiss and everyone tried to board the bus simultaneously. The driver shouted his usual string of expletives as at least half a dozen of the boarders offered badly faked bus passes or attempted to sneak aboard by ducking in behind the crowd in order to save their bus fare for ciggy money.

'It's fuckin' DT's mate! You're having illucidations.' His friend Scoddy informed him as they sat together amidst the bedlam. 'You need to cut down on the cider.'

'Fuck off, I only had half a bottle.' Daniel replied. 'I wasn't even that pissed!'

'No, honest.' Scoddy insisted. 'My uncle Wally got them on new year's day last year. He was sitting in the garden and his whole body started shaking. He threw hisself into the fuckin' pond!'

The bus stopped to let more children on.

'Oi! Numb nuts!' Trina called out to Daniel from the back of the bus. 'How come I've got one of your books in my bag?' She pulled out the exercise book and threw it across the bus, hitting him squarely in the face.

He woke up again.

Daniel daren't move. That last dream episode, like the previous ones, had been totally convincing. He didn't know now whether he was awake or not. His mother screamed from downstairs...

The rest of the day rolled past without event but Daniel habitually pinched his forearms in case he was dreaming. By lunchtime his skin had become reddened and bruised.

Gay Dave the drama teacher, who wasn't actually gay but was an effeminate thespian which is close enough for a class full of fifteen year olds, had noticed the marks on Daniel's arms during the lesson, and being a Childline volunteer in his spare time had approached him about them.

'It's called lucid dreaming.' Dave told him after hearing Daniel's story. 'It's when a dream is so lifelike that you can't tell the difference between it and reality.' He then went on about how, at fifteen Daniel's body and brain were developing and that a lot of changes were taking place and that if he needed to talk about anything his office was always open. Daniel nodded, half turning toward the door. There was no way he was going to be stuck in a room alone with gay Dave talking about how hairy his balls were getting.

'So don't worry about it.' Dave called after him as he left. 'Just don't fall off anything high.'

'What?' Daniel asked glancing back over his shoulder.

'It's just folklore.' Dave laughed. 'If you fall in a dream and you don't wake up before you hit the ground, apparently you die.'

'Great!' Daniel replied, smiling. 'Fucking great.' He finished under his breath, but at least now he knew what was happening, well, he knew what it was called and that's a start.

Double English finished off the school day. Daniel decided to walk home from school. He went via Turnsteads Road because that's where the public library was.

He felt uneasy as he entered the huge old building, primarily because he'd never been there before. He roamed around the bookshelves for perhaps half an hour without a clue until a middle aged lady librarian, who was convinced that he was up to no good, approached him.

'Are you looking for anything in particular young man?' She'd asked him, peering over her glasses as if he were something that had fallen out of her nose and into her prawn cocktail.

'Er... Got anything on dreaming missus?' He replied, for some reason trying to appear less intelligent than he actually was.

She beckoned and Daniel followed. There were at least two dozen books on the subject but there was one in particular entirely devoted to lucid dreaming, what it was, and how to do it. He had to fill a form in to join the library but at least he got to take the book home with him.

One of the 'cider club' had called him up on his cell phone just after tea. He declined their invitation feigning illness because he wanted to read. He disappeared to bed early, taking the book with him.

Gay Dave had been wrong.

According to the book, a lucid dream is one in which the dreamer becomes aware that he is dreaming but the dream still continues. Apparently this opens up all kinds of opportunities for experience, usually of a sexual nature, since the highly creative subconscious mind becomes one big playground and the emotional body is free to run rampant, unfettered by the ego. Daniel wasn't sure what it all meant but as a fifteen year old boy the idea of dream shagging captured his imagination like nothing else.

The book said that lucidity is often triggered by the realisation that something impossible had happened which engaged the conscious process just enough to wake the dreamer.

He also read an account of a monk who had cultivated the art of lucid dreaming and had become trapped in one of his own dreams. The monk had suffered horrific burns to his face and hands and had endured two years of painful reconstructive surgery while all the time being aware that he was dreaming and being unable to wake up.

He read on through the night until all of the words became one. Eventually his eyes rolled back and flickered closed. It was four thirteen in the morning.

School the following day wasn't easy. He dragged his feet from classroom to classroom, half dead with fatigue, until the final showdown, double maths.

He sat at the back of the class, head nodding. The writing in his exercise book was just meaningless scrawl. He couldn't even stay between the feint ruled lines. His teacher Mr Noakes, possibly the most boring man in the world, rambled on in monotone about how many pies there were around the edge of a circle.

A screwed up piece of paper landed on Daniel's desk. Daniel's eyes doggedly traced the source of the projectile. It was Trina, sitting two rows forward and one to the left, wearing panties and a training bra. She sneered at him over her shoulder.

Daniel checked again squeezing his eyes shut and rubbing the sore lids with rough knuckles. He was right. Trina wasn't even in his year and she was sitting in his maths class in her underwear, and no-one else had even noticed.

He was dreaming. He had to be. He looked around him at how vivid everything seemed. It was just like the book had said, bright colours, totally realistic. He spotted Rachel Wilberforce at the front of the class. God he'd fancied her since junior school but ever since she'd sprouted tits that looked like zeppelins fighting for a parking space he'd been competing with seventeen year olds for a chance to chat her up. He'd had to resort to keeping her as a wanking fantasy.

This is it, he told himself, standing up and walking over to her. She looked at him quizzically. He asked her to stand up. She stood up. So far, so good. He put his hand up her skirt. She slapped him so hard his ears rung. The rest of the class were in hysterics and Mr Noakes went ballistic as Rachel sat down red faced and tearful.

'What the hell are you doing boy?' Mr Noakes shouted.

'I, er...' Daniel muttered.

Mr Noakes swung his arm and slapped Daniel hard around the back of the head.

He woke up, face down on his desk.

'Norris, ' Mr Noakes droned, 'would you like to repeat to the class what I've just said?'

Daniel lifted his head. A string of saliva tenuously connected the corner of his slack mouth to his exercise book.

'Wha..?' Daniel offered as the rest of the class collapsed into laughter.

Mr Noakes threw a piece of chalk, hitting Daniel between the eyes.

Daniel woke up.

He was in bed. It was seven forty five in the morning and he was numb with shock. His mother screamed his name from downstairs...

Now utterly confused, Daniel constantly checked his state of awareness. His right forearm was so bruised that he'd had to start on the left one. After that he'd have to start pinching somewhere else. He became sullen and withdrawn, unwilling to engage with his teachers or his friends. All he wanted to do was get through the day.

Once at home he continued to read his book which outlined several techniques to encourage the lucid dream state. There was nothing in it however addressing the issue of how to stop dreaming.

It was late in the evening. He was lying on his bed, ironically unable to sleep. Beside him on the floor was a dirty plate garnished with pizza crusts. His mind raced in circles while his heart kept pace with it and his dry eyes stung with fatigue. Uncharacteristically he decided to take a hot bath in an effort to relax.

He was too tall to submerge completely so his knobbly knees poked out through the surface of the warm soapy bathwater. He closed his eyes and relaxed as best he could, listening to the rhythmic dripping of the leaky cold tap.

He became vaguely aware of a sensation of movement in the water, like the flicking tail of a large fish. He opened his eyes in the brightness of the bathroom. All was as it should be.

Until it bit him.

Something large clamped a jagged mouth around the soft flesh of his inner thigh.

Daniel sat bolt upright, screaming loudly, gripping the sides of the bath as whatever it was attempted to pull him under the water. He slid along the bottom of the bath, the pain in his leg so severe that it denied any sincere attempt at retaliation. His hands were wet and soapy but he gripped hard to

65

the bath. The thing in the water pulled at him, twisting from side to side almost as if to tear a piece from him. As the water reached his chin he took a huge breath and submerged. Only the strength of his hands remained to prevent him from being taken, and after a few more seconds wrapped in subjective eternity, they too relented.

He wasn't in the bath any more. The water was dark, deathly cold and bottomless. Daniel stared desperately upward at the surface of the water as he sank. It was quiet now. The monster had gone.

His body stiff, he drifted ever downward into icy blackness. The surface was now miles above him it seemed. He held his breath desperately, knowing how futile an effort it was but unable to accept the inevitable.

He felt a slimy touch in the darkness as cold thick weeds caressed his naked legs. They held him there, motionless and terrified.

He became aware of others. His eyes were now closed against the blackness but he was still aware of them. Other people, trapped like him but long since dead. They floated in the stillness like pale grey balloons. Hundreds of naked men, women and children; putrid and half eaten by the endless swarms of things that burrow and squirm in the fathomless depths.

His lungs burned and bubbles leaked from his nose.

Don't breathe, don't breathe, his mind repeated in its agony. He screamed into the water and it rushed in to fill him. He could taste the rot from the others as it swept down his throat.

He woke up.

Lurching upward and gasping desperately he threw himself out of the bath and onto the bathroom floor, drenching everywhere with cold soapy water. He pulled himself up onto all fours coughing the remaining water from his throat. He grabbed a towel and wrapped it around his shoulders before dropping exhausted to the floor. He lay there for a further ten minutes breathing heavily, waiting for the shock to subside.

Finally ready to move he clambered unsteadily to his feet. He re-wrapped himself in the towel and reached into the bath to let the water out. He saw his reflected hand rise to meet his as he reached for the plug. It broke through the surface and grabbed him.

He woke up on his bed, chilled in the darkness. Sobbing gently he rolled aside and pulled his duvet over him, not bothering to undress.

When he regained consciousness the following morning the first thing he noticed was that it was ten past eight. The school bus left at eight thirty. Daniel leapt out of bed, initially confused that no-one had seen fit to scream the morning chorus at him. Luckily he was already dressed, although somewhat creased and smelling strongly of bed sweat.

He grabbed his school bag from the bottom post of the banister and rushed into the living room expecting the usual chaos.

Everyone was dead.

His father sat at the breakfast table, a half eaten slice of toast in one hand, the butter knife stuck firmly in his throat. He was still holding onto it, as if he'd done it himself.

His mother slumped face first into her cereal bowl which had overflowed blood and milk onto the table cloth. He went around behind her and gently lifted her head. Her mouth fell open and a thick swarm of flies burst out into the room. Daniel threw himself back, away from the mass of buzzing iridescent blue bodies that seemed intent on making their way into is nose and eyes. He waved his arms to beat them off and backed into the kitchen.

'Oh, hi Danny.' Trina called out to him. He turned slowly around.

Trina smiled at him. She was wearing panties and a training bra and holding a steak knife in her right hand.

'How cool is this then?' She asked him, dragging the knife across her abdomen. She cut deeply. Her intestines poked out through the slit.

Daniel swallowed hard, unable to take in what he was seeing. His mouth hung open.

'You think that was good?' She asked him. 'Watch this.' She cast the knife aside and placed her index finger in her mouth. She grinned widely and then bit the end off.

Daniel screamed, urine flowing down his legs. He turned and ran face first into the door frame.

He woke up in his bedroom, stiff with terror. His mother screamed his name from downstairs.

He leapt out of bed.

'Fuck, fuck, fucking bloody hell!' He ranted, stamping his feet and throwing his duvet aside. He was scared and angry. Scared that this shit would never end and angry at pissing the bed.

On the way to school, not knowing whether or not he was dreaming and no longer caring, he reached the conclusion that something was after him. A demon or ghost maybe, but definitely something evil. Whatever it was, it came for him while he slept and as hard as he tried there was no way that he could stay awake forever.

He stared out of the bus window. They were passing St Mary's church on the corner of Shirley Road. Daniel got up from his seat and demanded to be let off the bus, claiming travel sickness and threatening to vomit liberally all over the driver if he didn't comply.

He walked into the church through the huge arched doorway, staring up at the ornate vaulted ceilings and listening to the silence. He could smell the old wooden pews and feel the cold of the stone flagged floor through the soles of his trainers. He hadn't really known what to expect but he hadn't imagined the place to be empty.

He walked further in toward the altar. He looked at the font which was half full with cool clear water. Not being particularly religious but having seen enough vampire movies to know what holy water could do, he dipped in a finger and daubed a cross onto his forehead. He didn't feel particularly different so he scooped up a handful and drank it instead.

'Can I help you?' A voice behind him offered. Daniel looked around. There was a short fat bloke with thick glasses standing by the door. He had a small round sticking plaster on his chin where he'd cut himself shaving.

'Are you the vicar?' Daniel asked him.

No. I'm the verger.' The man replied. 'I look after the church and make sure that its available for people who need it. Do you need it?'

'What words do I say,' Daniel asked, 'from the Bible, to protect myself from demons and stuff?'

'From demons?' The verger asked with raised eyebrows. 'I'm afraid it takes a little more than just words if your demons are real. Fortunately they very rarely are.'

'So what do I do then?' Daniel pressed.

'Face them.' The verger suggested. 'Confront them without fear and they'll shrink away I promise you.'

'Yeah right.' Daniel muttered wiping away a tear. 'You've got no bloody idea mate.' He stormed off toward the door.

'You could try the Lords Prayer.' The verger called after him. Daniel stopped walking. 'I find that it helps me when things get out of hand. Please. Sit here, I'll show you.'

Daniel sat in a pew next to him. The verger put his hands together and closed his eyes. Daniel copied him.

'Now, repeat after me.' The verger began. 'Our Father...'

'Our Father,' Daniel repeated. He didn't know who this bloke was but he ought to brush his teeth more often. He could smell his breath as he spoke.

'Who art in Heaven...' The verger continued.

'Who art in Heaven.' Daniel echoed. The verger's halitosis had become overpowering. Daniel jumped as a hand touched his knee. He opened his eyes as the verger flicked his stinking tongue into Daniel's ear.

'What the fuck are you doing? You fucking perv!' Daniel shouted, pushing him off. The verger laughed manically and tried to grab him between the legs. Daniel shuffled back and out of the end of the pew. He ran down the aisle and out of the door, the verger's cackling laughter echoing after him.

It was dark outside. It shouldn't have been, but it was. Daniel ran for the churchyard gate feeling all the time that the verger may be running after him. The path to the gate seemed to stretch out endlessly before him as he ran, and the harder he ran, the further away it seemed to be. Either side of the path row upon row of graves paraded their tragedy before him. Some of the stones were broken, others were completely absent, leaving nothing but a mound of grass.

It may have been adrenaline or the darkness playing tricks in the corners of his eyes, but it seemed to Daniel that some of the mounds were moving. He dismissed the idea, still running for the gate. But now even the ones in front of him were changing, the grass rippling like thick carpet. Thick carpet with something underneath it trying to get out.

As he skidded to a halt, turning on the spot, terrified but desperate for some kind of reality check, one of the mounds burst open and a skeletal arm thrust out, feeling around in the night air.

All thought in Daniel's mind ceased, and for a brief moment everything around him seemed to stop. This wasn't right, Daniel thought to himself. This was fucking impossible.

'Fuck this! He shouted into the churchyard. 'Fuck this!' He screamed again, standing in the middle of the path with balled fists. 'This is where it stops! What the hell do you want with me?'

Something came for him. It was deep and dark. It rushed at him and swept him away.

***

Daniel was standing on the edge of an old stone bridge. He was leaning over the brink of an abyss as he turned to face his demon.

'You rang.' Trina smiled.

'You get the fuck out of my head.' Daniel shouted. 'I'm warning you, stay away.'

'Or what?' Trina asked, staring quizzically.

Daniel shuffled perilously close to the edge.

'Or I jump.' He threatened.

'I see.' Trina replied. 'And this affects me how?'

'If I hit the ground I die, if I don't hit the ground I wake up. Either way you lose. I'm not afraid of you any more.' Daniel was crying now, wiping away his tears with his free hand.

'Let me help you with that.' Trina shrugged lightly.

The edge of the wall crumbled away from under Daniel's feet. He dropped straight down but managed to turn his body quickly enough to grab the cold stone with both hands. Another piece crumbled away leaving him hanging only by his right arm.

He turned slightly to look below him into the blackness of the drop.

'I'm fucking warning you, you bitch!' He almost squealed. 'I'll fucking let go!'

Trina jumped lightly onto the wall.

'You just don't get it do you Daniel...' She smiled, peeling back each of his fingers as she spoke.

Daniel fell. He plunged into the darkness, staring back at Trina's smiling face and hearing her final words to him.

'... You're the dream that I'm trying to wake up from.'

Daniel hit the hard dirt bank between the stream and the dam.

Trina Norris awoke with a start in the dim light of her bedroom, afraid to move.

*****

The Swing.

'It is as I have said, and I've told you the truth Mr.
Jenkins.' A brown circular tea stain became
momentarily visible at the rim of Edgar Henry's
white bone china cup as it rattled around the saucer
in his nervous hand. 'I'm a collector.' He offered a
forced and superficial smile but Paul Jenkins
remained unconvinced.

'By collector, I take it you mean an obsessive
compulsive stalker who crawls about in people's
gardens at night scaring the shit out of innocent
women and children by staring in through the
windows?' He looked directly into Edgar Henry's
eyes. There was something hard behind them. Like
some kind of desperate used car salesman; his
handshake was a little too firm and his cologne a
little too strong, and his steel grey eyes and beaded
perspiration betrayed his fixed grimace. Edgar
Henry was hungry for something that Paul Jenkins
owned, and Paul had a wife and four kids to support.

'Well, yes,' Edgar winced, 'I see how it must appear
to you, but please believe me, it was never my
intention to….'

'Try telling that to Marion.' Paul interrupted, 'My
kids are still sleeping with the fucking lights on. If
she knew that I'd agreed to meet you she'd cut my
bloody nuts off!'

'And yet here you are.' Edgar's smile became almost sardonic. 'Why is that do you think?'

'Because I have something that you want.' Paul shrugged.

'And you are considering parting with it?' The smile transformed. It slipped into something genuine, an expression of hope, perhaps even longing.

'For the right price, maybe.' Paul nodded.

'But Paul... may I call you Paul?' Edgar asked, reaching out to the dull and badly chipped yellow Formica topped coffee table to retrieve his cheque book. Paul couldn't help noticing the thick layer of grime and dust that had built up on the table top as he watched Edgar's trembling hands grasp for the tatty rectangular book. 'I've said before that I'm not a rich man.' Judging by the state of the place, Paul was inclined to believe him. He'd seen some shit holes in his time but this one took first prize. He'd smelled the kitchen as soon as he stepped in through the front door, even above the suffocating stench of cat piss. How many fucking cats do you need to neglect to make a smell like this? He'd walked through the hallway, afraid to touch anything. He knew instinctively that every surface in the house was sticky and coated with cat hairs. He'd been offered tea, which he'd politely accepted, but there was no way on earth that he was going to drink it. Now he was sitting in a dirty, worn out armchair talking terms with a complete bloody madman. He kept feeling a slight flicking sensation on the skin of his hands and ankles as countless cat fleas gorged themselves on his lifeblood and then catapulted their bloated carcasses back into the rotting carpet.

'You offered me a thousand quid.' Paul stated blandly.

'A thousand, y...yes.' Edgar stammered, patting his pockets in search of a pen.

'Only it's five now, sorry.' Paul smiled.

'What?' Edgar looked momentarily shocked. 'Five thousand pounds?'

'Look mate, it's nothing personal. I've got a wife and four kids to feed.'

'Indeed.' Edgar sighed deeply. He opened the cheque book and found the first empty cheque. 'Very well.' He murmured, 'Five thousand it is.'

'Ten.' Paul snapped.

'Ten!' Edgar stared, aghast. 'Paul, I don't have ten thousand pounds.'

'But you'd pay it if you had wouldn't you?' Paul insisted. 'If you had the cash available to you you'd pay twice that amount, because you know something that I don't. You know how much it's really worth.'

'It's not about financial gain Paul.' Edgar whined. 'Believe me; nobody else on earth would give you more than ten pounds for it. It's personal, a family heirloom if you will. Please Paul, be reasonable.'

'Reasonable! Paul leaned forward, almost shouting. 'I'm being bloody reasonable! All I want is half of what it's really worth. I'll split it with you, straight down the middle, fifty-fifty. I'm not greedy Edgar. I just want what's mine, that's all.'

'What's yours?' Edgar stared, wide eyed. 'You want what's yours? And what is that exactly?' Edgar's face reddened. Traces of spit flew from his mouth as he spoke. Paul felt them land on his face and was suitably disgusted. 'How much did you pay for it? A few pounds perhaps? Or was it in the bottom of the box with a job lot left behind after a house clearance auction? Just how much did you pay?'

'It's just a key!' Paul glared. 'A fucking rusty old key! Yes, if you want the truth I paid the grand sum of two pounds for it because I thought it looked nice; sort of olde worlde and...'

'And now you've got it hanging from an old nail on one of the fake ceiling beams in your pathetic mock Tudor home with no concept of its intrinsic value.'

'That's right,' Paul nodded, speaking softly. 'You're absolutely right. I don't know what I have. But you do, and you're going to tell me or you're never going to see it again.'

There was a silence between them. A tunnel forged in the atmosphere by two pairs of eyes, locked upon each other. It was Edgar who spoke first.

'Very well,' he sighed, 'but you're going to be greatly disappointed.'

'Let me be the judge of that.' Paul half smiled.

Edgar slumped back onto the decayed and threadbare sofa. Paul felt slightly ill at the sight of the small plumes of dust that squirted from the splits in the upholstery. The cat piss smell grew stronger.

'The story begins about forty eight years ago, well, from my perspective at least. It actually goes back much further of course. My grandfather moved here from France in nineteen thirty eight bringing my six year old father with him and leaving his only brother, my great uncle Luke, behind. It is Luke that this story is really about. Of course, I didn't meet him until the one occasion that he came to England. He travelled about a lot you see. He was a magician.'

'What, you mean card tricks? Rabbits out of hats? That sort of thing?'

'Yes, yes exactly that sort of thing,' Edgar giggled, barely able to contain his obvious delight, 'rabbits out of hats, very good.' His eyes seemed to glaze over for a short time while his smile remained fixed, as if forgotten about. 'He worked as a butcher for some years, a job that was both strenuous and tedious, but all the time he was busy planning. Designing tricks and illusions, that was his obsession. He was about twenty five years old when he finally decided that the time was right to take the stage. He actually did quite well for himself in the early years. He was muscular and handsome, quite debonair in

76

many ways and when he performed he did his job well. He hit problems, as did everyone, when the Second World War began. Living in an occupied country crippled the morale of the entire population. You'd imagine, wouldn't you, that people would seek out entertainment to distract their attention from the horrors around them. In Luke's case however it would seem not. But still he planned. He planned, designed and constructed ever more complex, elaborate and baffling illusions. It's been said that Albert Einstein produced his greatest work while employed as a patents clerk. Luke was working in a meat processing factory but in his own field he was no less a genius.' Edgar paused as if waiting for some kind of response.

'And?' Paul prompted. 'Where does my antique key come into it? Any time soon?'

'You have to be patient Paul, as I have been for many years. If you only knew...'

'Fine,' Paul shrugged, 'give me a nudge if I fall asleep.' He feigned indifference. If he remained detached he could drive a harder deal. Edgar appeared unmoved by Paul's sarcasm.

'After the war he started up again, training his young wife Gabrielle as his assistant. But the world had changed, hardened. He stated his feelings quite eloquently in a letter to Grandfather when he said: "My audience has transformed from a garden of roses into a crown of thorns." They worked hard in those days and were poorly rewarded. It was several years before Luke realised the truth; that people needed more than simple entertainment. They needed to be moved, thrilled... scared.'

'Scared?' Paul scoffed openly. 'They'd just survived a world fucking war! Why the hell would they need to be scared?'

'Who knows?' Edgar shrugged. 'Perhaps it was because they'd just spent almost seven years under constant threat and now they were simply enduring the daily drudge of trying to rebuild their lives. In comparison to the past few years they were now living in monochrome and yearning for colour.'

'And Great uncle Luke could give it to them, right?'

'Right.' Edgar nodded. 'He developed a stage performance entitled "Contes d'Obscurité". It roughly translates as "Tales of Darkness". It was noted by the critics of his day as a most hypnotic mix of the beautiful, the gory and the truly macabre. The audiences lapped it up and he became quite famous, although perhaps infamous would be a better adjective. His show was, in the main, just a rework of standard illusions and slight of hand with a few spooky effects, a little fake blood and some screaming thrown in. There was one illusion however that captured the public's imagination so much more than the others. It was called, "The Swing".

'Can't say I've heard of it.' Paul admitted, secretly feeling as if he ought to have.

'No.' Edgar shook his head. 'I wouldn't expect it. You're too young. I was privileged to witness perhaps the last ever performance. I was five or six years old and although the show wasn't entirely appropriate for children grandfather wouldn't have let me miss it. We had to sit right at the back, unnoticed.'

Edgar paused again, the dissociated vacant sheen returned to overshadow his eyes.

'It was Blackpool Tower Circus, forty eight years ago.' He continued. 'The high wire ballerina had just finished when the lights went out. We were in pitch darkness for a good two minutes until a small white light flickered on over the centre of the ring, and there it was... the swing. It was surreally beautiful. A wooden swing; free standing on a small platform. The framework was painted white and decorated with entwined roses that were such a pale pink that their colour could almost have been imagined. It had sturdy looking ropes and a simple firm wooden plank for the seat. Then as a slow waltz drifted up from the orchestra two figures appeared on the edge of the darkness. Circling softly in unison, the man embracing his partner closely, they danced smoothly together around the circle of light. They were dressed in immaculate fashion. He as a soldier in best dress complete with ceremonial sword; and she in a stunning ball gown, pink, like the roses. They wore white porcelain masks decorated with fine featured faces in black and gold. She had blood red lips and he had a fine black moustache. After two or three minutes of breathtaking dance they finally approach the swing. He grasps her delicate waist and gently lifts her onto the seat. She appears coy as he takes each of her hands in turn, kisses it gently and places it on the swing rope. He walks around to the back and pushes her softly. She swings freely to the music.'

Edgar, his eyes closed and his smile wide, swayed with her for a few seconds while Paul watched, feeling strangely uncomfortable, like some kind of voyeur. Edgar's face suddenly darkened.

'Then there is a change in the air.' Edgar's breath quickened. 'Perhaps it is the lighting but it seems suddenly cold. The music becomes a cacophony, a huge mound of discord that climbs and climbs until it can't go any further. There is a white flash of lightening and a roar of thunder as the soldiers face changes to a mask of anger, hers to one of unadorned fear. It transpires that he is the devil himself acting from beneath a semblance of true love. But it doesn't end there because it slowly dawns upon the spellbound audience that although she is still swinging... and has been swinging throughout... her legs are no longer visible. The devil moves around to the front and pulls away her dress and there is nothing, nothing at all. She is still on the swing but the seat is at her waist. Her lower half is completely missing. The devil holds his sides and laughs as her face again changes. She pleads in silence. Her mouth is open and distorted; her eyes are wide with shock. He draws his sword and dances manically around her thrusting the blade into the empty space beneath the swing. Thrashing and hacking he dances and laughs while her fixed porcelain face silently begs for release. In the end she screams and as she finally dies, the lights go out.'

'And then everyone gets put back together and all is forgiven I suppose.' Paul offered, pretending to stifle a yawn.

'Well, yes, but not as part of the trick.' Edgar pointed out. 'It was essential for the macabre image that the victim remained dead. But yes, after a short spell of darkness the light came back on and the swing was gone but great uncle Luke and great aunt Gabrielle stood hand in hand, restored to their former beauty. They remove their masks, take a bow and then waltz away into the shadows to rapturous applause.'

'Sounds good,' Paul nodded, after a short pause. 'If you're interested in that sort of thing. Not exactly David Copperfield though is it?'

'What?' Edgar raised his silver white eyebrows.

'Well, it sounds to me like a glorified version of the old "sawing the lady in half" trick, but with a bit more class though, I'll admit.' He'd started the sentence in a self assured manner but had felt the need to temper it toward the end because Edgar's face was morphing before his eyes from incredulity, via contempt, to pissed off.

'What?' Edgar burst into scornful laughter. Paul actually began to feel threatened. 'The old sawing a woman in half trick?' There were tears in his eyes. 'Good God man there's no comparison! Absolutely no comparison.'

'Look, I never said I was an expert.' Paul cleared his throat. 'But if you have to be one to appreciate his work then surely it's not about entertainment any more, and that defeats the object of performing in the first place.' Edgar's expression mellowed as he considered Paul's words. He stood in thought for far longer than Paul considered necessary for such a minor point. It supported his initial premise that Edgar was a few pence short of a quid.

'Right.' Edgar sighed. 'You're right. Perhaps, if you will allow, I can give you a brief education... '

'Look,' Paul interjected. 'I'm not here to criticise your interests. It's just... '

'The half man illusion,' Edgar began, speaking loudly over Paul's moderate voice, 'has been performed for over a century in various forms. In its simplest expression, often seen in Middle American sideshows, it comprises of a single man, or rather the upper half of him, perched on a table which appears, although dimly lit, to be fully open to view. The trick is one of the earliest forms of mirror magic and entails the use of a large mirror sitting at a forty five degree angle under the table facing the floor. The audience, whose viewing angle is strictly controlled, believe that they are looking through the underneath of the table whereas they are actually seeing a reflection of the front two table legs and the floor. The lower body of the half man lies, somewhat uncomfortably, behind the mirror and provided that the floor is featureless and the side views obscured, the effect is really quite striking.' Edgar broke into spontaneous giggles. Paul watched him, saying nothing. 'But here's the problem, and the defining issue that separates common stage magic from its superior form. With the half man illusion the audience viewpoint is fixed and the set must remain stationary or it becomes immediately apparent how the feat is accomplished. The swing however remains in motion throughout the entire performance and the audience has a viewing perspective of a full three hundred and sixty degrees. So you see, there really is no comparison.'

'So... How did he do it then?' Paul asked softly. Edgar just stared at him. 'The moving version.' Paul prompted. 'How did he manage it?' Edgar continued to stare and then slowly leaned forward. Cat piss and cologne invaded Paul's nose as Edgar whispered.

'Exactly.'

'What! You mean... you don't know?'

Edgar laughed loudly, planting a fat hairy hand on Paul's shoulder.

'No one does! That's the whole point!'

'Well, yes I know that... a magician never reveals his secrets etcetera. But after he died; didn't he leave his equipment to anyone? His wife maybe, or another magician?'

'No.' Edgar shrugged. 'On the contrary, he actually went to enormous lengths to conceal his methods. His will was quite specific in that respect. His solicitors were instructed not only to disperse his props far and wide amongst various branches of my family but also that certain contractors were to be employed to carefully dismantle everything so that it could be distributed even further.' Edgar's eyes dropped. His artificial smile strained to breaking point, the corners of his mouth quivered. 'That's why it's taken me over twenty years to get it all back together.'

'You've found it?' Now Paul's eyes were wide. 'All of it?'

'Almost all of it yes.' Edgar nodded. 'Except for a few small but vitally important items.'

'My key?' Paul suggested. Edgar didn't answer. 'You need my key to complete something, to make it work, right?'

'Yes.' Edgar whispered.

'It's the swing isn't it? Paul added softly.

'Yes, yes it is.' Edgar closed his eyes tightly but despite his efforts a single tear escaped, running down the side of his nose. 'You've no idea how hard it's been.'

Paul had made a resolution before he'd arrived. Don't get involved. Don't sympathise or it'll cost. He was out to make a deal, to get as much for the key as possible. Perhaps Edgar was right, maybe didn't deserve it, but who the hell said that life was fair?

'And how much is the working model worth as opposed to the non-working one?'

'I've already said it's not about money.' Edgar sniffed. 'It's about family. It's about giving a brilliant illusionist the recognition that he deserves, and to some extent it's about being the only one in the world who knows a family secret. I'll never sell it.'

Paul suddenly found himself on the back foot. How do you negotiate with an idealist? How do you prise cash from the pocket of someone who harbours a completely alien set of priorities? He'd have to play a waiting game. Sympathise and pretend to be interested, and then hype up the situation until his key became something indispensable.

'So, er, where is it? Paul asked tentatively. Edgar just looked at him. 'Come on mate, we've come this far.' Paul put his hand on Edgar's shoulder. He was hoping that Edgar wouldn't spot his insincerity, he wasn't a good actor. Edgar continued to stare.

After a long moment Edgar seemed to suddenly wilt. Then he spoke quietly.

'Seven thousand.'

'What?'

'I'll give you seven thousand pounds for that key. It's all that I have, believe me.' Now it was Paul's turn to stare. He was sorely tempted to take the cash and leave the mental bastard to it, but something inside told him that there was more to be had here. How did he know that he wasn't being conned. He'd seen the programs on TV with the

snotty antiques experts lording it over some
disappointed old bag that's brought some of her old
granddad's toys in for valuation. 'Oh yes Missus
Johnson, if it had been in the original box it would
be worth fifty thousand pounds. But as it is...' pause
for dramatic effect, '...three pounds fifty.' It's the
details that make the difference. How could he be
sure that Edgar didn't have a rich collector waiting
in the sidelines? He had to take it further, to make
Edgar even more desperate.

'I want to see it first.' Paul stated quietly. 'I want
to know how it works. Then the key's yours, for
seven grand.'

Edgar turned away. Paul watched his back,
silently urging him to accept. He aimed his thoughts
like daggers into Edgar's slightly kyphotic spine.
Eventually Edgar seemed to return to the room.
Paul feigned indifference, but held his breath.

'You have to promise me.' Edgar whispered, 'that
what you learn will never be told or spoken of to
another living soul.' Paul couldn't suppress the urge
to giggle.

'Magicians honour.' Paul grinned. Edgar just
stared. 'Sorry,' Paul grimaced, 'I didn't mean to
laugh. It's how I cope with tense situations. I won't
tell anyone. You have my word.'

'Thank you,' Edgar sighed, 'and now, if you'll follow
me.' He turned and walked briskly away, speaking
over his shoulder as he went. 'You know, I actually
feel quite relieved, as if a burden shared is a burden
halved.' Paul followed quickly as Edgar lead him out
through the back door of the house.

Fresh air had never smelled so sweet. It's
surprising what your brain can learn to ignore. The
cat piss stench was now perhaps even more
memorable in its absence. They walked along a
driveway toward a building that resembled a double
garage. The heavy steel door rattled loudly as Edgar
leaned against it, searching in a trouser pocket for a

bunch of keys. He removed a large padlock from the hasp embedded in the concrete driveway and threw the door upward with a grunt. The door rolled up, grating loudly as Edgar ducked his head and entered. Paul followed him but stopped short as the fluorescent tube lighting flickered to life.

When Paul was a small child he'd been taken to a museum. Apart from all of the exhibits, which mainly comprised stuffed animals, old armour and ancient gilt pottery, the really great thing about the huge rambling old house was the freedom that it afforded. Every single room was open to him as he ran from one to the other, racing between the exhibits, his small brown leather shoes beating loudly on the polished wood floors. Nobody scolded him, nobody cared. He ran without restraint for over half an hour until he came to a door that was locked. He'd twisted the dull brass doorknob with sweaty palms and leaned hard against it, but it didn't move. He barged at it with his shoulder, his outrage mounting as it held fast against him. Eventually his mother had tugged him away by the arm, whispering angrily into his ear while roughly straightening his clothing.

'It's private.' She'd hissed, yanking at the sleeves of his jacket.

'What's in there?' He'd shouted, twisting out of her grip. He craned his neck to look over her shoulder at the dark oak door as she crouched down beside him.

'I don't know,' she'd snapped. 'It's probably full of things that they don't want people to see.' Paul pulled free of her and ran off. Whenever he'd caught the smell of brass he'd been reminded of that door. The smell of the old doorknob had stained his small hands. He could smell it over the top of the ice cream that his mother had bought him later that same day and taste its lingering acrid flavour on the thumb that he sucked in bed that night.

He'd often wondered what was behind that door. He'd envisioned many possibilities, all of them conveniently reflecting whatever fantasy had currently suited his age, but if anything had ever come close it surely had to be what he was seeing now.

This room was the home of obsession. Clean, tidy and superbly organised, it had floor to ceiling shelving, packed with overflowing box files, the contents of which he could only guess at. There was an immaculate tool chest with every shining piece in place situated half way along the side wall and what appeared to be a microfiche screen in one corner. There were old framed pictures on the walls, yellowing posters advertising long dead stage acts offering genuine feats of amazement and wonder. A large central poster took pride of place on the back wall. It showed a young, strong man in evening dress standing alone and gesticulating in some mysterious fashion before a small audience. His shadow was dark red and shaped like the devil. The text, in blood red, said 'Luc Enrie - Contes d'obscurité'.

The room was warm and carpeted. There was a small and very tidy kitchen unit in the far corner, equipped with clean cups and a shining silver electric kettle. In the middle of the room were several boxes, an old trunk, and some kind of large contraption which was wholly concealed under a huge dust sheet.

'As I'm sure you can see now,' Edgar half smiled, 'this is where I actually live. The house is a place that I rarely use. I sleep here most nights, on a pull out bed.' He gestured toward a small sofa. 'This is my life's work, finding great uncle Luke and bringing him back.' Paul didn't answer. He hoped that this would be sufficient prompt for Edgar to continue. God knows how long he'd been dying to tell someone about his achievements, his little secret. Paul didn't have to wait very long.

'I have copies of the records of every theatre in France since nineteen twenty.' He pointed to the endless rows of stuffed box files. 'I have microfiche copies of all of the local newspapers of the time which I've searched for theatrical advertisements of his act. I have an extensive genealogy tracing all of my relatives, several hundred would you believe, and the original copy of Luke's will and that of his wife, which details the disposal of his props. I have travelled throughout Europe in search of everything that you see here, and as far as I'm aware I have almost all of it.'

'Almost.' Paul nodded.

Edgar stepped slowly to the centre of the room and reached down to grab the corner of the dustsheet. He pulled slowly. The sheet slid away to reveal the swing. The paintwork was cracked and peeling and there was evidence of damp staining on the bottom corners of the base. It was, on the whole, quite unimpressive. Paul felt somehow cheated. He'd expected so much more.

'Wonderful isn't it?' Edgar beamed.

'Er, fantastic.' Paul offered weakly.

'The whole device is designed to be pulled apart for transportation and then reassembled very quickly. Everything just slots together and then locks into place with these latches.' Edgar pointed to several well camouflaged iron bolts. 'And of course it's been done in such away that even when it's in pieces nobody can tell how it actually works... Marvellous!'

'And you've really no idea at all?' Paul asked.

'I have my suspicions,' Edgar mused, 'but I'm fairly sure that it's been booby trapped so I can't confirm anything.'

'Booby trapped?' Paul asked.

'Oh, nothing dangerous.' Edgar assured him. 'It was common practice to protect magical props in such a way that if a rival ever managed to disassemble them they'd never go back together again, so you see...' His sentence trailed off into a deep sigh.

'You're not trying to rob me at all are you?' Paul grimaced.

'What?' Edgar asked, as if the very idea offended him.

'You actually mean what you're saying, when you go on about all this,' Paul shrugged, 'and the key that you're after, my key, it's not worth anything to anyone but you.'

'It's as I've said all along.' Edgar nodded slowly.

Paul let his eyes float over the swing. The chipped paintwork and decrepit woodwork betrayed it for what it was. A relic from a bygone age. Something which, even if it wasn't actually dangerous, would probably never work again. Only someone like Edgar could look at it through rose coloured glasses and fool himself into believing the hype. There was nothing more here for him. He gave up.

'Seven thousand five hundred and the key's yours.' Paul grunted.

'I don't have that much.' Edgar shrugged.

'Then you'll have to wait until you do.' Paul replied.

Edgar seemed to sag inwardly. He buried his face in his hands and shuddered. Paul could sense his inner turmoil. Somewhere in there a decision was being made. Paul crossed his fingers for luck as Edgar looked into his eyes.

'Very well.' Edgar sighed. 'Seven thousand five hundred it is. But I want you to go home and bring it back here today.'

'No need.' Paul grinned. 'I've brought it with me!'

'You... You've got it?' Edgar stammered. His eyes seemed to involuntarily search all of Paul's visible pockets for key shaped lumps and bumps.

'It's in the car.' Paul added. 'I'll go and get it while you're writing the cheque.' He turned for the door as Edgar searched his pockets frantically for a pen.

As Paul approached his car his excitement mounted at the prospect of getting hold of some serious cash and finally paying off all that shit that they'd mounted up on the credit cards over last Christmas. He could buy a new game console for the kids perhaps. Maybe even a holiday. He pressed a button on his key fob and the car bleeped and the lights flashed. There was a smug clunk as the doors unlocked.

He reached into the passenger side door and pulled open the dashboard glove compartment. The key slid forward and he scooped it up. A wave of doubt welled up inside him as he slammed the car door closed.

It had occurred to him that once Edgar had the key in his possession there would be nothing to stop him from ringing his bank and cancelling the cheque. If he asked Edgar to wait for the key until the cheque had cleared he risked Edgar having second thoughts about the deal, so the transaction had to go through while Edgar was still hyped up about it. What he needed then, was some kind of insurance policy. A lever that was worth more to Edgar than the money he'd paid for the key. A solution dropped into his mind almost immediately and he mentally patted himself on the back for being such a cunning bastard.

As he pushed open the door to the garage, Edgar greeted him with an expectant smile.

'I've made us some more tea.' Edgar explained, pointing over to the tiny kitchen area. On the work surface were two very clean looking pot mugs and a small steaming teapot. 'It's Earl Grey,' he added, 'not that tasteless supermarket rubbish that you had earlier. This is a celebration.'

'I have one further condition.' Paul spat quickly. Edgar's face froze immediately. 'What's to stop you

cancelling the cheque once you have my key?' Paul
asked.

'I... Well I... ' Edgar spluttered. 'I just wouldn't.'

'But you could though couldn't you?' Paul pressed.
'So I thought that I should wait here and we'll
discover your little secret together.'

'What? No!' Edgar wailed. 'That's not part of our
agreement. It's unacceptable. I... '

'And, ' Paul interrupted, 'if you let the payment go
through, you have my word that nobody else will
ever find out, whereas If you stiff me I'll unleash the
power of the internet on you, and every fucker and
his mother will get to know about it.'

Edgar turned away. He'd imagined it was over.
He'd looked forward to this moment for over twenty
years. The moment when all of his work and
relentless research finally bore fruit. There should
have been no sweeter taste than this, but there was
a fly in his soup. A greedy and undeserving blight
that stained the satin white fabric of his success.
There was one more hurdle. Another one of the
thousands that he'd already overcome to get to this
point. Just one more...

'Agreed.' Edgar sighed, unsmiling. 'May I have the
key now?' He asked.

Paul pulled the heavy and tarnished key from his
pocket and waived it tantalisingly in Edgar's face.
Edgar's eyes followed it like those of an insanely
eager puppy expecting a ball to be thrown.

'May I have the cheque now?' He answered.

'Yes,' Edgar mumbled, retrieving it from the pocket
of his beige woollen cardigan. He handed it over for
Paul to inspect. Paul unfolded it and scrutinised it
carefully for mistakes or omissions. He took so long
that Edgar began to feel insulted.

'The key please.' Edgar prompted. Paul shrugged
and dropped it into his hand.

Edgar caught the key as if it were on fire. He walked over to the swing carrying it as if it were something infinitely fragile. Paul almost laughed.

'Don't worry, it won't break.' He quipped.

'Sorry?' Edgar answered, barely able to pull his eyes away from the key.

'The key,' Paul explained, 'you're holding it like its Jesus Christ's left nut!'

'Or the Holy Grail perhaps?' Edgar suggested smiling widely. Paul didn't know what he was talking about so he kept quiet and took a seat on the sofa bed.

There were several keyholes in the base, all well concealed to the casual glance. The key, Edgar knew, fitted all of them.

'The key to this, if you'll excuse the pun,' Edgar declared walking around the swing, 'is in triggering the locks in the correct order.' He stood back a couple of paces taking the object in as a whole. 'I've done some degree of research, looking at the plans for the device, and I believe I know the sequence.' He walked off to the kitchen work surface and brought back a tray replete with mugs and teapot.

'This has to be done very carefully.' Edgar warned, filling each mug from the steaming teapot. 'The secrets of this prop are well guarded. One wrong move and we'll never get it to work.' He handed one of the mugs to Paul, who accepted it with a nod.

Edgar went back to the swing and bent over the base examining one of the corners. With his thumb he slid aside a tiny panel that concealed a keyhole. He inserted the key and holding his breath, he turned it. There was a quiet whirring sound and a dull thud, and a further concealed panel bumped open revealing a small hole. Edgar giggled softly.

'What was that?' Paul asked, sipping his tea. It tasted a little bitter. He considered asking for some more sugar but then thought better of it. It was Earl bloody Grey after all.

'It's all part of Uncle Luke's genius.' Edgar explained, still giggling. 'The whole thing is clockwork! We have to wind it up.' He lifted a flap on the top of the base and pulled out a heavy looking iron lever which he slotted neatly into the hole. He grunted loudly as he forced the mechanism to turn for the first time in decades.

Paul watched him struggle as he sipped his tea. Counting almost subconsciously he estimated approximately one hundred and twenty four turns before the contraption refused to go any further.

Edgar pulled out the lever and set it aside. He stood up and breathing heavily he wiped the perspiration from his face with his sleeve.

'What happens now?' Paul asked, barely interested.

'Well, if I'm not mistaken,' Edgar wheezed, 'there's another lock to open and then the mechanism should start.' He pulled the key from the first keyhole and then placed it into another which was half way up one of the vertical beams. He turned it easily but nothing happened. He stood back, a puzzled look spread over his moist face.

'Well?' Paul prompted.

'I... I'm not entirely sure.' Edgar admitted. 'I feel certain that the swing was supposed to start moving.'

'But that wouldn't look right would it?' Paul suggested. He finished the last dregs of his tea and then stood up. 'I mean, a swing doesn't just swing on its own does it?' He walked over to the swing and grabbed one of the dirty grey ropes. Very gently he pushed it forward. The wooden seat swung back and forth and continued long after common sense would expect it to have stopped. Edgar giggled again.

'Well done! Oh well done!' Edgar laughed. 'Now, you see that small cog up there in the cross beam?' Paul looked up and then nodded. 'It has exactly seventy two teeth, and each full oscillation of the swing knocks it round by one tooth. The frequency of the swing suggests that it will take about a minute for the cog to go completely around.'

'And then what?' Paul asked.

'Who knows?' Edgar shrugged.

Paul went back to his seat. As the swing drifted lazily back and forth he seemed to move with it. Its slow oscillation relaxed him.

'Any moment now.' Edgar warned.

All at once there was a loud snapping sound from the simple wooden plank that formed the seat of the swing, quickly followed by a loud clap as a formerly secret panel in the base flashed open and then closed. A frenzied whirring noise erupted from inside the base taking several seconds to grind to a halt.

'And that's it.' Edgar sighed.

'What do you mean that's it?' Paul asked, making himself comfortable. 'Nothing happened!'

'Au contraire.' Edgar argued solemnly. 'Absolutely everything happened.'

'I don't suppose you'd like to elaborate?' Paul smiled. He was really beginning to feel on top of things, sort of in control.

Edgar pulled the key from the keyhole and then took it around to the back of the platform to insert it into yet another one. As he turned it a large panel bumped open. Edgar lifted the panel and peered inside. He paused for several seconds before sitting back on the floor and wiping his heavily sweating brow with his arm. He stared at nothing.

'Well?' Paul asked.

'You see.' Edgar began. 'When it comes right down to it there are really only two types of stage illusion. The first kind endeavours to convince the audience that something is happening when in fact it isn't. The second kind attempts to fool the viewer into believing that nothing is happening when it actually is.' He got up from the floor and lurched over to a small chair. He sat down and rubbed his face with his hands. 'On this occasion it would seem that Uncle Luke adopted the latter approach.'

'I've no bloody idea what the hell you're talking about.' Paul admitted.

'He had many secrets.' Edgar sniffed. 'All this,' he said, gesturing to the room in general, 'isn't really that relevant. The things that I've learned, over all these years, about how he performed his illusions, have been mere pointers, hints at the possibility of another secret, one that goes far beyond even my expectations. And the swing, it just proves that my suspicions are justified.'

'Suspicions?' Paul prompted.

'It began about six years ago.' Edgar mumbled. 'I was reading all the old newspapers on the microfiche, looking for adverts for Uncle Luke's act when I noticed something odd. It seemed more than coincidence that all of the personal columns had missing persons notices in them. Notices primarily about young women, missing from towns that Uncle Luke had previously visited and furthermore the number of missing women matched exactly with the number of performances that uncle Luke gave, in every single case. Nobody else would have noticed this of course because they'd have had to look back to where he'd been rather than where he was now or where he was going next. I had the luxury of being able to see everything at once in retrospect and so I was able to make the connection.'

'What exactly are you saying here?' Paul asked. He couldn't seem to follow Edgar's logic.

'What I'm saying, ' Edgar replied, 'is that, although there was illusion, there was no magic. I'm saying that the blood was real, the screams were real and the death was real. I'm saying that my great uncle Luke was a serial killer and that he ruthlessly slaughtered helpless women several times a week before a paying audience and that not one of them ever suspected.'

'You're bloody joking!' Paul gasped.

'I wish I were.' Edgar grimaced. 'The next clue was in the collection of dresses that Luke had in the props wardrobe.' Edgar pulled himself out of the chair and walked over to a large wooden trunk which he opened, revealing several pale pink ball gowns. He selected a single gown and threw it on the sofa bed next to Paul. 'You see that they're all identical but for the fact that they're in a range of sizes. Why would that be do you think, if it was always Aunt Gabrielle who acted as his assistant?' He walked over to the kitchen work surface and brought back a small box which contained perhaps twelve small bottles. 'Several months ago I came across another piece of the puzzle.' He explained. 'The recipe for a simple toxin that Uncle Luke would slip to the girl of his choice in order to ensure her compliance. I've taken the liberty of adding some to your tea, I hope you don't mind.'

Paul grinned inanely at Edgar's last comment. Nevertheless when he tried to move he found that he couldn't. His body simply held its posture. Even his face seemed to be set in stone.

'The final clue resides within the swing itself.' Edgar continued. 'That snapping sound that it made was the rapid retraction of a fine wire loop which is more than capable of cutting someone cleanly in two at the waist. I assume that the lower half of the poor unfortunate victim would fall into a trap door below the swing while the audience was distracted by the music and the lighting. Inside the base is a maceration device composed of hundreds of interlocking blades that would reduce muscle and bone to mince in a matter of seconds. Remember the whirring noise toward the end? Presumably Uncle Luke would have disposed of the upper body in much the same way after the show.'

Paul remained completely motionless as Edgar moved toward him.

'If you'd have taken seven thousand for the key instead of trying to squeeze every last drop out of me I wouldn't have had to do this, so you've only your own pointless greed to blame.' Edgar leaned over Paul's unresponsive body and began to unbutton his shirt. 'The real test of course is to see the thing in action. Then there can be no question that the secret that Uncle Luke fought so hard to protect had absolutely nothing to do with his stage show. How much do you weigh Paul?' Edgar asked. 'I've picked out the biggest dress for you. Oh I do hope it fits.'

*****

Doing it for Isaac.

A wave of nausea and a thumping headache were the first things that Hanna became aware of. On top of those sensations were stacked various additional levels of discomfort that could be attributed to having spent several hours slumped unconscious in a hard wooden chair, held firmly immobile by twenty or more layers of silver duct tape which fastened her bare forearms to the arms of the chair and her equally bare shins to the legs of it.

She opened her eyes and then slowly lifted her head. Her neck was painfully stiff and her vision was blurred. Where were her glasses? Her ears picked out the ticking of several large clocks and from somewhere in the distance, beyond the walls of the room, came the rattling bark of a dog.

Hanna turned her head slowly and screwed up her eyes in an effort to squeeze some sharpness into her vision. Her dizziness seemed to be easing slightly. She inhaled deeply to combat the remaining sickness in her stomach but began to cough spasmodically as runny mucous slurped up into the back of her nose and caught in her throat. She fought to regain control of her chest which was heaving for want of air. It was a difficult process compounded by the fact that her mouth was taped over.

She blew hard down her nose, forcing it clear. She could feel the stream of warm mucous hanging from her chin. What little of it was left in her nose, she snorted up and swallowed. It tasted metallic, like blood.

There were clocks everywhere it seemed. At least two dozen of varying diameters lined the walls, each possessing a bland white face set with Roman numerals. To Hanna's less than perfect eyesight it was either ten minutes to two, or ten past ten.

She turned her head the other way, trying to take in her surroundings. It was a very large room, appearing by the thick beams and exposed stonework to be some kind of barn conversion. She sighed in frustration. She could be anywhere.

Taking a deep breath, she pulled hard against the duct tape. She winced in pain as countless fine hairs were torn from the skin of her forearms but still she continued to pull. She pulled and writhed and jerked from side to side until her head felt as if it would split from the effort, but the tape held firmly enough for the realisation to dawn on her that she couldn't win. She sagged. Her eyes swam with stinging tears and a slight sob escaped her throat.

The car park.

Her last memory before waking up here had been the car park outside of work. It was almost dark when she'd finally left the office and bundled her bits and pieces into the boot of the car. The rest of the car park was empty. Hanna pressed a button on her key fob and her car blipped and flashed its readiness. She dropped into the driver's seat, fired her up and reversed slowly out of the parking bay. There was a dull thud as she eased backward and the bonnet dropped slightly on the right side.

'Bollocks!' She'd spat into the damp air as she threw the door open. The right front tyre was completely flat.

She stormed to the back of the car and opened the boot to pull out the bottle jack and the wheel brace. The spare wheel was, thankfully, serviceable and after something of a struggle she had it out of the boot and leaning up against the side of the car and was therefore left with the next hurdle; weak arms and tight wheel nuts.

Another car swung smoothly into the car park. Hanna mentally acknowledged its arrival but then gave it no further thought. This car park, although private, was commonly used by the public in the evenings and on weekends. The car eased into a bay some distance to her right as she leaned hard on the wheel brace. She grunted softly, applying all of her strength. As she jolted it with her bodyweight the wheel brace twisted in her grip and slipped off the nut, slamming her fists hard into the cold tarmac. She yelped loudly and then swore equally loudly. The knuckles of both hands were scraped, bleeding and dirty. One of her false thumb nails had detached completely, raising another exasperated curse.

'You look as if you're in need of a man.' A male voice offered quietly from several metres away.

'Just my bloody luck.' Hanna muttered to herself, attempting to cradle each hand simultaneously in the other. All she needed was a bloody smart arse trying to exploit her situation. She ignored him.

'Excuse me.' The voice came again.

'No thanks!' She called out with falsified cheeriness and without turning to face him. 'I'll deal with it.' She waved a very sore hand in the air in dismissal and then glanced around for the wheel brace which seemed to have bounced under the car. She heard dull footsteps fading away into the distance. Night had fallen fully by now and the car park was poorly lit. As if by dark conspiracy at that moment it began to rain. Hanna looked at her hands. 'Oh, what the hell. Why not?' She sighed to herself, turning around.

'Wait!' She shouted. The footsteps stopped. 'Please. You're right. I can't get the bloody wheel off.'

The footsteps returned quickly and the shadows parted to reveal a tall, slim man wearing a black Krombie overcoat, a white shirt, faded blue jeans and black leather brogues. He had long black hair, swept back tightly into a pony tail, revealing thick dark eyebrows, even darker eyes and a firm angular jaw line. Hanna had suddenly begun to consider the possibility that the evening may not be a complete disaster after all.

'The spanner thing...' Hanna began, knowing what it was called but playing the part. 'It's gone under the car.' The man approached slowly as Hanna turned and squatted down to retrieve the wheel brace. It hadn't gone far. It had tucked itself on the inside of the front wheel. She reached under to get it and her hand brushed against something else. Something sharp. She grasped it gently and pulled it out. It looked like several two inch nails, welded together at the head to form a ball of outward facing spikes. 'Look at this.' Hanna spat standing up. 'Some poxy bastard has deliberately...'

The force of his attack overwhelmed her. She was knocked over the bonnet of the car, and as she sprawled face down over it he grabbed a handful of her hair and repeatedly banged the side of her head against the cold metal before covering her nose and mouth with a cloth. There was a sickly sweet, gaseous smell. It carried her away.

And when she awoke...

How long had she been unconscious? She looked for a window. All of the curtains had been closed but there still seemed to be blackness behind them. Hanna concluded that it was still night time, but this wasn't much help. She looked down at herself. She was still wearing her panties and bra but the rest of her clothes were gone. What else had he done while she was out cold? She couldn't feel any vaginal or rectal pain but then again, she was in so much discomfort everywhere else that a bit of fanny bruising would be small game by comparison.

It's hard to scream down your nose, but she tried it anyway. She started coughing again. What the hell had he doped her with? Her nose felt as if she'd been snorting tequila. Her eyes started streaming. She blinked hard to clear them.

There was a sound behind her. Hanna's body went rigid. She whimpered down her nose, forcing her head as far round to the right as she could, but she couldn't see anything. She heard it again. It sounded for all the world like someone stirring a cup of tea.

'Ah, I see you're back with us.' A male voice said from somewhere behind her. She strained again to turn her head as he came into the field of her peripheral vision and then moved back out of sight. He was teasing her, the mad bastard. Hannah screamed her frustration.

After perhaps thirty seconds he came back into view, walking with teacup in hand, around in front of her.

He picked up a small wooden stool and placed it just a few inches from her badly scraped knees. He kicked a leg over it and sat down facing her, placing his steaming cup of tea on the carpet beside him.

'I imagine that you have a few questions.' He said softly. Hanna didn't respond. She simply stared at him.

'I've been through your handbag so I know who you are and where you live.' He smiled, pointing out a tubular steel coffee table to his left onto which he'd tipped all of the contents of her bag. 'Oh and I've managed to save these for you.' He fished around in his trouser pocket and pulled out her glasses. 'The frame's a bit twisted and the right lens was badly cracked when they hit the car bonnet and bounced onto the floor.' He opened the frame and pushed them gently onto her face. Hanna shook her head, throwing them off into her lap. He sighed deeply and picked them up.

'I have a large staple gun in my coat pocket.' He informed her. 'Let me assure you that if you do that again I'll staple them to your head.' He slid the glasses back into position. This time Hanna didn't move.

'That's better now isn't it?' He grinned, leaning over to the table to grab her small compact mirror which he held up to her face.

Hanna looked at herself. She saw her retro style horn-rimmed glasses, tilted obliquely on her face and with several large cracks in the right lens. The right side of her face was badly swollen and discoloured and what little mascara she normally used was now smeared down both cheeks. Her nose was thickened and split at the bridge and had been bleeding. There were several dry scabs peeling from her nostrils and a strip of silver duct tape over her mouth. It was strung with snot and blood and the sick fuck had drawn a distorted smile on it with a black marker pen. He'd even gone to the trouble of drawing in the teeth with the centremost upper incisors blacked out.

'Doesn't that make a pretty picture?' He grinned. Hanna began to throw herself back and forth, heaving madly at her restraints. The man sat back slightly and stared at her frenzied efforts as if she were a bondage show. He looked almost bored.

'I admire your efforts Hanna,' he sighed, placing a gentle hand on her knee. She felt the sting of his touch on her raw skin. 'I really do, but you can't get out of this...'

Hanna stopped struggling. Hearing him say her name, speaking softly to her like an old friend, in this context. It was like being hit in the stomach.

'Believe me, I know,' he continued, 'I've done it all before.'

It was a simple enough statement. Simple and yet enormous in its implications where Hanna was concerned. She began to sob.

The man picked up his tea cup and took a sip, sighing with satisfaction.

'And you should consider yourself quite lucky that I brought the duct tape.' He reached into his left coat pocket and pulled out a large silver staple gun. 'I was going to use this.' He fired a couple off in her direction. One of them bounced off of her naked stomach leaving a stinging white mark that soon turned an angry bluish-red.

'My name is Richard Evans.' He told her. 'Doctor Richard Evans actually, and it's my real name. There's no point in hiding anything because I know how this is going to end.'

Hanna was crying now. Head down, blinded with tears and barely able to breathe, she moaned rhythmically as her mind withdrew.

Richard leaned forward and placed a finger under her chin to lift her head. He drew back, suddenly disgusted at the rivulets of blood stained mucous that clung to his hand. He spotted a box of tissues on the coffee table and plucked one out to wipe his fingers before reaching out, grabbing a fist full of Hanna's ash blonde hair and yanking back her head.

'I need your attention Hanna.' Richard insisted, trying to lock his eyes onto hers. She stared blankly into nowhere. 'You have to know that none of this is my fault. That I... we... have no choice. It's all to do with Isaac Newton.'

Hanna drifted back to him, her mind still crippled by shock and chloroform. She didn't know anyone called Newton. It must be mistaken identity or something. She hadn't done anything wrong. Certainly nothing to deserve this. What the hell was he talking about? Of course he had a bloody choice! And if she could get him to take this fucking tape off her face she may be able to convince him to let her go. Sit up and try to pay attention she told herself. Try to make a connection with the mad sod.

Although Richard was still gripping her hair, she nodded slightly. He let go.

He sat back a little on the stool and nodded his approval as Hanna fixed her sight firmly on his face.

He glanced around the room, as if looking for a place to start.

'Hanna,' He said finally, 'do you believe in destiny?'

Hanna almost laughed. He's gone to all this trouble to deliver a cheesy fucking chat up line. She shook her head.

'Well, you should.' Richard stated softly. 'Because it is your destiny to die by my hand and it is my destiny to kill you.'

Hanna shook her head again, violently this time, ignoring the splitting pain.

'Of course you disagree.' Richard explained. 'So has everyone else that I've put in your position. But it will make no difference.' Hanna stared at him. 'In the past six years I have killed eighteen people. I've never been caught, obviously, despite the fact that I've made very little effort to cover my tracks. The police haven't even realised that there's a serial killer operating. This is because they look for modus operandii whereas I use a completely random method every time.' He began to chuckle.

'God.' He laughed, wiping a fake tear from his eye. 'What irony that is.' He sniffed and shuffled on the stool.

'Anyway, down to business.' He rubbed his hands together almost gleefully. 'As I said, I'm no stranger to this so I'm fairly sure how the argument would develop if you were able to join in. The first few times I went through it all in detail out of courtesy but it's remarkable how similarly people think when they're in your situation, so I just developed an FAQ list.' He took a deep breath. 'As the victim your primary duty is to yourself so your first question is inevitably, why me? Well it's just the way it is.' He shrugged. 'Perhaps the question should be, why anyone? Do you know how many hunter gatherer societies believe that the predator and the prey are spiritually connected? That the prey actually agrees to die in order to support the predator?'

Hanna shook her head. This was fucking ridiculous. People didn't choose to be victims. But she also knew that people did. Her sister ended up in a women's refuge because her husband kept beating her. She put up with it for years. Even after she left the refuge, after her ribs healed up, she still went back to the sad bastard. But not her. She'd have knifed him or waited until he was asleep and then put a large potato in a long sock and swung it into his fat face.

'Virtually all of them.' Richard stated. 'It didn't seem reasonable to me either at first, but you have to look at the big picture to see how it all hangs together. '

He shuffled again on the stool. The dry joints where the round wooden legs inserted squeaked as he moved.

'I was driving home from work one evening, passing a bus stop with a large queue of people, when a front wheel bearing disintegrated and the passenger side wheel turned out to the left. The whole car swung over, mounted the kerb and ploughed into the bus stop. I didn't have time to react. One man died instantly and two others were crippled for life. The whole thing was thoroughly investigated of course but there was no room for blame. It was just bad luck.'

Hanna's attention returned to the room. She'd been distracted halfway through his little speech by the urge to urinate. She was just past the twingeing phase and into the constant bladder ache. Richard leaned toward her. The stool creaked. She felt his mood change, as if the room had become suddenly colder.

'But let me tell you,' He said solemnly, 'killing someone isn't easy to come to terms with. I couldn't sleep, eat or even think straight for months. My only distraction lay in my books. Physics, maths and mechanical engineering. I read them over and over for days on end. Memorising every line, reworking every calculation a thousand times until I could do them purely in my head. One evening as I pored over Newton's principle laws of motion for the umpteenth time, something occurred to me and however I looked at it I couldn't produce a counter argument. It was the notion that Newton's combined laws of causality imply that free will is an illusion and that as a result it's effectively destiny that governs our whole existence. '

Hanna wasn't listening. She shuffled in her seat, trying to suppress her ever increasing urge to urinate.

'You see,' he said, steepling his fingers, 'the laws of motion state clearly that a body can do nothing more than that which is imposed by the sum of the forces acting on it. This means that nothing, absolutely nothing, is random and that every state is the result of every other state that has gone before. Yes the interaction is complex, immensely so, but essentially, if you had the computing power, you could capture the initial state at the moment of the big bang and by following the path of every single particle, predict everything that has happened since, and by extension everything that ever will. So you see, Isaac Newton has a lot to answer for. He's inadvertently aligned scientific thought with the concept of fate, formerly considered to be conflicting paradigms, and in so doing he's eradicated good and evil and the associated concept of sin. Quite an achievement don't you think?'

He paused slightly, shifting his weight and becoming irritated as the loose joints in the stool creaked loudly.

'The real point is Hanna, that every choice you've ever made was never a choice at all. Every thought you have ever had was the product of every other and so on, like an endless row of falling dominoes. We spend pointless lives acting out Newton's grand play like plump little automata with neither influence or implication, and the fact that I will kill you is no more my choice than anything else I've ever done. I put the stinger under the wheel of your car, that much is true, but when you refused my help I walked away. Why did you then call me back Hanna? Why did you invite me into your life?'

He leaned toward her, his breath smelled of strong sweet tea as he spoke softly into her ear.

'Destiny.' He whispered. Then he sat back, frowning deeply.

'I clung onto the idea for months,' he continued, 'to the exclusion of all else really, eventually I reached the conclusion that just as it was that man's fate to be killed, it was my destiny to kill him. I am living evidence of Newton's grandest theory, but then of course, that's all it ever would be, a theory, unless some brave pioneer, someone like me, actually puts it to the test by applying scientific principle. And so that's what I do. I play my part, anonymously of course, killing repeatedly in the name of science, gathering evidence as it were, and you're a part of it all. Surely something so enormous is worth dying for?'

Hanna didn't even hear the question. The bloke was a nutter! How do you negotiate with a nutter? Especially when you're bound and gagged! It was no good. She couldn't hold it in any more. The pain in her bladder had become intolerable. She squealed in frustration and then let it go. Yellow brown urine oozed out through the fabric of her panties, pooled on the seat of the chair and then poured onto the carpet. Richard looked at her, disgust clearly visible in his expression. Saying nothing, he stood up and walked off behind her. She toyed with the notion that he may have gone off for a towel or something, to wipe up the mess and dry her off. Instead he returned several minutes later with a large canvas duffle bag.

'Your next question should be, will he spare my life?' Richard began fumbling with the drawstring. 'But I think we've covered that one already so I'll move on to the third question which is, how will he do it?' He opened the bag and pulled out a long thick rope. Hanna fought to push herself backwards, as if to disappear into the back of the chair, as his eyes began searching the exposed overhead beams for somewhere to tie it up. He moved the rope through his hands until he found one end. He paused, holding the end of the rope toward his face and then turned to Hanna. He moved the end of the rope towards her, winding it back and forth like the head of a snake, making hissing sounds. When he got to her face he hissed again darting it at her. Hanna didn't blink. She just stared him in the eyes. He was an arsehole, and she'd met enough arseholes in her time to be able to tell him that without using words. She glared at him, and he understood.

'Time to bring this to a conclusion I think.' He said, turning back to the beams. 'I've picked a very soft rope you'll be please to hear. I'm not the kind of man to inflict undue pain on a woman. Not like poor old Frank, or number seven as I call him. That was a tough job. I went on a mission to break every single bone in his body with a hammer. I started with his toes, then his fingers, working my way up to the large bones. The smallest bones are in the inner ear. I had to use a screwdriver to get to them. All in all it took about an hour to kill him and a further two to

finish the job. Don't let anyone tell you that
scientific research is easy.'

'Ah!' He grinned, picking a point on an overhead
lateral beam. 'This'll do fine.' He threw one end of
the rope over and caught it, and after tying a slip
knot onto the remaining length he pulled it tight to
the beam. 'You have to be careful with this kind of
thing.' He explained while he worked. 'The beam has
to be thick enough to stand the drop as well as the
body weight. According to Newton, a body will exert
a reaction, by virtue of the covalent bonds that hold
the atoms and molecules together, that is equal and
opposite to the force applied to it. But if there's
insufficient energy available to maintain rigidity the
body will deform, exhibiting an elasticity modulus
appropriate to the type of material, which if
surpassed will result in plasticity, in this case
breaking the beam.' He turned to face her. 'Have you
ever seen how a noose is tied?' Hanna shook her
head. 'It's very simple. I looked it up on the net. I'll
show you.'

He pushed back some of the larger items of
furniture to give himself space and then pulled the
coffee table into the centre of the room under the
rope. He grunted as he pushed it. The glass top was
perhaps half an inch thick, making the table much
heavier than he'd anticipated. He brushed all of
Hanna's possessions aside, stepped up onto the table
and measured off the height of the rope where the
noose should be.

'Too low.' He stated blandly. He stepped down and
picked up the stool, which he placed on top of the
table. He stepped onto the table and then stood on
the stool. He looked down, nodding to himself. He
gathered up the rope and made three folds in it,
then set about wrapping the folds together with
thirteen small loops.

'Thirteen loops.' He said aloud. 'It's always thirteen loops by tradition because it's an unlucky number. Some people are just fucking sick!'

He pulled a penknife out of his pocket and with some degree of effort managed to cut off the trailing length. He turned slowly on the stool, taking tiny steps, until he stood facing Hanna. He was grinning almost sardonically.

'Nearly there.' He said, opening the noose. He popped his head through the large loop and began pulling faces at her.

'Boo!' He shouted, staring wide eyed. Hanna had had enough of his crap. She rolled her eyes to let him know how fucking tedious his little jokes were becoming. A flicker of malice crossed his face.

'I know you're angry Hanna,' Richard grimaced, 'but I intend to spare you any pain by using the chloroform first. However, if you wish to continue with your little petulant frenzy I'll be happy to miss that part out.'

As far as Hanna was concerned angry didn't even come fucking close. A fair fight was all she wanted... and something to stab him with.

Richard grabbed the loop in both hands and tugged down hard as both a test and a threat. A shower of thick dust fell from the beam coating his shoulders like pale brown dandruff. Richard wafted it away from his face with one hand but couldn't stifle a violent sneeze that forced his body to buckle. He brought his throat down hard on the loop and reflexively jerked his head back away from the pain and as Isaac Newton would have it, the large shift in mass solicited an equal and opposite reaction in the stool which proved sufficient to surpass the frictional coefficient of its loose and ill fitting leg joint.

The stool collapsed.

The drop wasn't enough to break his neck but as Hanna gaped in disbelief the bastard hung there choking. Richard kicked out his legs, trying to find anything nearby to support his weight, but there was nothing.

Hanna almost squealed. Incredulous and relieved, salty tears filled her eyes as she witnessed the utter panic etched into Richard's scarlet face. His expression suddenly changed, as if a realisation had dawned upon him. Hanna glanced around trying to see what he'd seen. Then she looked up. The rope was soft and the slip knot, true to its name, was slowly slipping.

Richard pointed his toes directly down toward the coffee table. Hanna estimated the clearance to be about twelve inches. At the rate that the knot was sliding he'd be able to support himself in about a minute. All he had to do was last that long. His fingers were still trapped under his throat and he dare not try to take them out for fear of pulling the already painfully tight noose even tighter. He tried working his head gently from side to side in a vain effort to free the carotid arteries. His breath came in heavy gasps. He felt as if his larynx were being crushed, but the knot was slipping. All he had to do was stay conscious, and wait.

Hanna's heart sank. Maybe it was her destiny after all. Maybe she'd had been waiting for the bastard all her life. But on the other hand...

...Maybe he'd been waiting for her.

She threw her body from side to side, pushing her hips forward. The chair jumped forwards and sideways. She had about fifty seconds to push the coffee table aside which would add a further minute and a half to his descent. Surely to God he couldn't last that long!

She jerked again, more to the left this time. Richard looked on through bulging bloodshot eyes as her chair leaned and finally tipped over. Hanna's head slammed against the floor forcing a guttural gasp down her nose. Her mind was flooded with pain and her vision tunnelled. She tried to breathe deeply, desperate to hold everything together, but the shadows closed slowly across her mind's eye.

The sound of a rattling gasp pulled her back to reality after... how long? Her heart leapt as her mind rapidly brought itself up to date. She lifted her head and saw Richard's toes still hovering above the table. There was now barely three inches of clearance.

Hanna glanced up at his face. It was distorted and blue and his manically glaring eyes were weeping blood tinged tears that rolled down his cheeks and dripped from the tip of his chin, but he was still very much alive.

Despite the agony in her head she thrust her hips forward. The chair jumped. She thrust again and again. Eyes closed, ignoring the pain and the crippling effort, she pushed on with grim and singular determination.

Richard had maybe two inches left to drop. There were bright silver jagged slashes across his vision where the retinal blood vessels had burst. His heart pounded in his ears and his dry and swollen tongue filled his mouth so that it made a grating sound when he tried to breathe around it. His larynx ached intolerably and his arms had become numb and limp due to the pressure of the rope impinging the nerves in his neck. His only objectives were to breathe and to wait. Not long now, he repeated internally, like a survival mantra. Not long now.

Hanna felt the cold steel of the table leg touch her naked stomach. It was the single, most joyful experience of her life. Now spurred on she attacked her plan with renewed vigour. Thrusting forward she inched the table aside with her abdomen. Her final backbreaking thrust brushing the tubular frame from beneath the tip of Richard's leather shoe.

He desperately tried to kick out a leg, to regain the table somehow, but lack of oxygen had weakened him and nerve impingement forced crippling bolts of pain down his spine.

He couldn't wait any longer. He couldn't last for another two minutes while the knot slid through far enough to deliver him to the floor. He had no choice now but to try to force it. His only remaining hope was that his body had sufficient strength left for the task.

He drew in as deep a breath as he could. His dry tongue clung to the inside of his mouth making even the smallest inhalation a monumental effort. He lifted his legs slightly, almost imperceptibly, and dropped them. The pain in his throat seemed to increase tenfold and he felt the skin of his neck begin to tear. He repeated the movement, trying to accelerate the slip of the knot.

Hanna, from her position below him, could see what he couldn't. There was no more than an inch of rope left to go. After that he would fall, and shortly thereafter she assumed, he would recover enough to be able to finish her, and she was fairly certain now that chloroform wasn't an option.

Richard jolted his body again. Gasping and choking he sprayed mucous from his nose. His throat creaked and squealed as he forced air back and forth through his deformed larynx.

He has to die, Hanna prayed inwardly. After all this, surely he has to die.

The knot slipped.

Hanna watched him fall. Almost in slow motion he dropped straight down. His leg caught the edge of her over turned chair as he fell, deflecting his body sideways. She closed her eyes as he tipped backwards. His body too weak to support him he landed on the frame of the coffee table. His upper body hit the thick glass top which promptly imploded.

After a few silent seconds Hanna opened her eyes.

Richard was lying beside her. Unable to move he simply stared, his eyes still bulging and his face a blackish blue. A huge shard of glass had entered the side of his neck and exited through his mouth wedging it wide open, impaling his tongue and shattering several of his teeth en route.

He began to laugh. His bloodshot eyes rolling madly in their sockets. Hanna's stomach heaved as spatters of hot blood hit her face. He laughed the guttural, cackling laughter of the insane. It was the sound of a man who had won the hardest possible battle only to find that he had lost the war.

The laughter stopped.

Hanna had never watched anyone actually die before. She found it both horrifying and oddly beautiful.

She began to laugh, and she began to cry.

*****

Home from home.

It was pissing down again. The rain was
hammering so hard that Maria could barely see
through the car windscreen despite having the
wipers on full tilt. She pressed on through the
horrendous conditions, moving cautiously along the
badly drained B road looking for anything that
resembled the entrance to a driveway.

The solicitor had said that the house was set well
back off the road but that it couldn't be missed
because it was the only property for miles that still
had any of the old woodlands surrounding it. She
was also told that it was atmospheric and quaint
which, reading between the lines, Maria had taken
to mean strange and possibly spooky.

She spotted the turn off on her right. A brown
green blur of old trees that suddenly seemed to part
in the middle. If this was their idea of a driveway
then the previous owners must have gotten around
on horseback. Maria felt a little guilty for her lack of
gratitude but after all she hadn't even known them
and in all honesty to receive a letter out of the blue
informing you that someone you didn't know existed
had left you a house, well, it's just a bit too good to
be true.

The foul weather began to finally ease off as she
rolled the car gently along the dirt track. As the
woodlands thickened everything seemed to become

suddenly dim. Maria turned off the windscreen
wipers and switched on her sidelights. The tree
canopy was so dense now that the last vestiges of
rain barely made it through. She drove on for a
further three or four minutes before finally spotting
the house. She stopped the car about thirty yards
from the front door and got out.

She slammed the car door closed and stood a while,
looking at the ramshackle building. It was
picturesque certainly. It stood in a small clearing, its
off white walls made bold by a warming shaft of
light that had managed to force itself between the
clouds. Too large to be described as a cottage and yet
not big enough to be a family home, it was a
property developer's dream, and that's what Maria
was.

The real beauty of this place, Maria thought to
herself as she stepped along the brickwork garden
path, was that it was a brown field site. This meant
that the local council would have no objection to her
demolishing it and building a more suitable habitat
in its place. This house wasn't worth anything. It
had neither gas nor electricity and probably no
sewer or piped water but it came with five acres of
woodland and she could almost certainly put
something good here. With some investment this
place could be worth a fortune.

There would be a key under a stone to the right of
the front door. Maria found it and made her way
inside.

To her disappointment the house was empty. For
some reason she'd expected it to be full of furniture.
She could visualise everything in its proper place as
she walked from room to room. The kitchen should
have an old Aga stove decked out with black cast
iron pots and pans, and bunched herbs hanging from
a wooden rack fastened to the ceiling. She could
almost smell them. The tiny living room should have
a rocking chair set beside the fireplace, and a cat,

curled in slumber and purring loudly in the heat of the coal fire.

There were two bedrooms upstairs. The dry wooden steps creaked as she ascended. Again Maria saw in her mind's eye all those things that were missing. The small wooden beds and the tired and threadbare woollen carpets. The exposed ceiling beams that sagged with age. There was no bathroom. The toilet block was outside in the back garden, probably feeding straight into a cesspit.

She'd never been here before, and yet there was such familiarity, so much, well, comfort in the place.

She had to shoulder the back door open to get out into the small herb garden. It was severely overgrown and had been thoroughly infiltrated by weeds but she could still pick out its former glory. There was lavender, rosemary, comfrey and even the coltsfoot had managed to keep hold by spreading its wide cobweb covered leaves out over the cracked stone path. And there were foxgloves, valerian, St John's wort and snake plantain and... How did she know all this? The closest she'd ever been to a herb garden was buying evening primrose oil from the local health food store to ease the pain in her tits during her period. She'd never even bothered to take that regularly either.

This should have freaked her out, but it didn't. On the contrary it made her feel warm inside, as if she'd just sunk a neat double malt whisky. She went back into the house and wandered around a little more, enjoying the sensations of somehow belonging.

Maria wasn't naturally sentimental. Oh, she remembered people's birthdays and had wiped away a tear over the closing scenes of Titanic but that was about it. She didn't even cry at her own wedding. But it would be a shame to knock this place down, she thought. This old house, so full of love.

She glanced at her watch.

'Good god!' She gasped aloud, almost running for the door. Three hours. She'd been here for three hours! How the hell had that happened?

As she drove off she found herself repeatedly glancing at the house through her rear view mirror. She almost stopped the car for a last look. It wasn't until she solemnly promised herself that she'd come back tomorrow that the house finally let her leave.

As her husband Rob snored the night away beside her, Maria's thoughts floated back to the decrepit building. Its effect on her didn't seem as strong now that she was away from it but it still belonged to her. It really, actually, belonged to her in a way that money can't possibly buy. Rob would be disappointed, Maria thought, that she wasn't going to demolish it. She was going to renovate it. And they were going to live there.

It would be counter productive, Maria thought as soon as she opened her eyes early the following morning, to introduce Rob or the twins to the house in its present state. She'd have to spend a little time on it first, to clean it up and make it a bit more promising.

Rob went off to work. Maria dropped the girls off at primary school and then headed home. She bundled all the cleaning kit that she could find, a radio, a folding chair and a packed lunch into the car and sped off to her new project.

As soon as she turned onto the dirt track she began to smile. When the house came into view she positively squealed with delight. Before entering she filled a large plastic drum with water from the stream that ran behind the house. Once inside she donned the rubber gloves, rolled up her sleeves and set to work.

She cleaned the entire place from the top down as someone would groom a favourite pet. She spoke softly to it as she wiped the grime from the windows. She hummed soothing tunes as she swept the cracked and splintered stairs. She didn't even stop to eat lunch.

After several hours she considered round one to be over. There was still a lot to do but the cleansing of the house was more of a symbolic affair than a genuine effort at improvement. It was a kind of bonding. Yes that's it, Maria smiled. They were bonding.

Suddenly tired, Maria set out her folding chair in the kitchen and pumped a cup full of hot coffee from her thermos flask. She sat down with a sigh and relaxed. It was two o'clock. She had to pick up the kids at three.

She rested there for a few minutes until a faint rumbling sound caught her attention. She listened intently. The sound came again. It was coming from the living room. Maria stood up and walked from the kitchen, her ears aching for sounds. As she entered the living room the noise erupted again but this time it was accompanied by the frenzied mewling of a cat. She listened hard. There! Sounds of feline panic once again filled the room, but from where?

Under the floorboards? Maria gasped as the rumbling began again. There was a cat under the floorboards! Impossible Maria thought, and yet...

She ran to the car and pulled out the bottle jack. The lever was flat on one end. Certainly flat enough to insert between these ageing warped planks. She pushed the lever deep between the shrunken boards and pulled hard. The floorboard creaked angrily and then gave way, almost flying up into the air. Maria peered into the gap.

'Puss, puss.' She called softly. 'Here puss.'

To Maria's frustration there was nothing there. No cat, no rabbits, rats, nothing. But she did notice something quite odd.

Maria was no stranger to renovation and she'd seen under a few floors in her time. Mostly they were either dry earth or clay beds. Especially in the really old houses. This one was unusual however. In this case it was:

'Glass?' Maria asked aloud. She put a hand through the gap in the boards. It was dusty, yes, and uneven, but unmistakeably glass. Thick, dark green, bottle glass.

This was something special Maria concluded. This was a genuine feature. A glass floor. She set to work pulling up the rest of the boards. It was no great shakes. She'd have had to replace them anyway.

Having removed several square metres of flooring she stood in the middle of the room, broom in hand. She swept away the surface dust and was intrigued to discover some kind of pattern etched into the glass. She set about it with a cloth and detergent, following the lines around until they finally returned to where she'd begun.

Circles within circles. Three concentric rings.

That's it? Maria thought. Just three circles?

Maybe there was more in the middle she reasoned, reaching for the soap sudded cloth. She washed away the accumulated dirt and grime of decades, her work area becoming bigger and bigger as she scrubbed. There was no more to the pattern than she'd already found but in the centre of the floor was a patch of glass that appeared paler than the rest.

The surface was so rough that it was impossible to actually see through no matter how hard she tried. An idea occurred to her. Perhaps if she wet the surface? Maria pulled the bowl of water toward her and tipped the soapy contents out onto the glass. As she wiped aside the bubbles and stared into the floor her heart leapt into her mouth.

There was a face looking back at her.

It was blurred and distorted by the uneven thickness of the glass but unmistakably female and about Maria's age. Maria leaned closer, trembling visibly. Her adrenalin knotted stomach burned as she pressed her own face against the floor only half believing what she was seeing. As she once again wiped the surface of the glass with her shaking hand, the face came into sharper view and its eyes flicked open.

Maria was still screaming when she awoke, sitting in her fold up chair in the kitchen.

'A dream!' She gasped into the darkness. 'A fucking dream!'

She noticed then how dark it was and ran for the car. She grabbed her cell phone from the glove box.

Seven missed calls. Four from the kid's school and three from Rob. It was nine thirty in the evening. She'd been asleep for over seven hours.

The following morning Rob was still moody about her forgetting to pick up the twins. Maria didn't mind that much because despite having slept away all of the previous evening and also managing to sleep soundly through the night, she still felt as if she'd just walked a thousand miles. Rob would come around. He always did.

It was Friday, Maria reminded herself. She'd give the house a miss today and take Rob and the girls there tomorrow. She dropped the twins off at school and then came home, ate breakfast, and fell asleep on the sofa.

Saturday morning could have been better. The girls woke up in a foul mood and Rob was of little help. He just kept wondering what all the rush was about as Maria packed the boot of the car with food, spare clothes and the small, easy pitch tent that they'd bought last summer but never actually used beyond the front garden wall. The forecast predicted fine, warm weather and they had enough land around the old house to hold a Woodstock revival so why not make use of it? Maria jammed the sleeping bags into the car boot and forced it shut.

Oblivious to the riot that was going on around her Maria drove stoically to her destination. The bedlam fell silent as they approached the house.

'Where are we mummy?' Jemma asked. She was the youngest twin by eighteen minutes and had felt a relentless desire to catch up with her sister ever since.

Rob looked at Maria, his expression silently asking the same question.

'Well,' Maria explained, 'if all goes to plan, this is our new home.'

'But it's so creepy.' Lulu pitched in.

'Nonsense.' Maria answered, opening the car door and getting out.

'Thanks for discussing that.' Rob muttered under his breath while climbing out of the passenger side. He walked quickly to Maria who was already striding down the path.

'Lulu's right you know.' He said quietly. 'This place gives me the willies.'

'Well throw a couple my way when you get the time.' Maria answered curtly.

The girls had caught up by now. They were standing behind Rob on the front doorstep. Lulu leaned in through the door and looked around.

'It smells.' She announced, wrinkling her nose. 'And I bet there's spiders and stuff.'

'No spiders.' Maria called from the living room. 'Come and see.'

Both girls stepped cautiously over the threshold and then ran inside.

Rob was as thick skinned as they come but this place felt like the closing moments of a football match in which Millwall had just lost, three - nil. There was a serious and unmistakable atmosphere of threat. He went in anyway.

The thunderous row coming from upstairs was a firm indication that the twins had shaken off their previous trepidation in favour of fighting over bedroom space. Surely Maria hadn't intended that they live in it as is, Rob thought, glancing around the tiny living room at the warped floors, cracked walls and sagging ceiling. The place was barely standing up let alone fit for habitation. There wasn't even a shitter for God's sake!

They should pull it down and start again, Rob concluded, and even then it might be hard to live here. Some places just feel negative.

'Don't worry,' Maria smiled walking in from the kitchen, 'I felt the same at first.' She handed him a steaming hot coffee. 'It'll grow on you, you'll see.'

Yeah, Rob thought, like athlete's foot.

'I suppose you've got a million and one ideas for the place?' Rob asked accepting the hot drink.

'I need to inspect it a bit more thoroughly yet.' Maria answered. 'I want to save as much of it as I can. Let's go upstairs and look in the roof space.' She turned away heading for the stairs. Rob followed on, silently hoping that a colony of bats had taken up residence. You could do most things with a site like this, but if you discover a protected species you may as well knock your plans on the head right there.

As they reached the landing they could hear the twins whispering frantically. Maria looked at Rob through raised eyebrows. It doesn't take much parental experience to know when your kids are planning something. Maria and Rob sneaked up to the flaking bedroom door and peered inside. Both girls instantly turned to face them.

'Can we keep him mummy?' Lulu begged.

'Pleeeeeeease mummy,' Jemma added, 'we'll look after him.'

They were sitting facing each other in the middle of the floor. Between them was a huge and very dirty looking black cat. It rolled onto its back purring loudly as several large red fleas scuttled for cover in the sparse pale fur of its round fat belly.

Maria approached the massive feline and rubbed its chin with her finger. The animal mewled in ecstasy.

'He's a lovely fat fellow isn't he?' Maria smiled. 'But we don't know who he belongs to so we can't keep him.' The twins groaned in unison. 'But you never know,' Maria added, 'if we're especially kind to him he may keep coming to visit.'

His name's Greediguts.' Lulu announced.

'Very fitting.' Rob remarked approaching the animal which suddenly leapt to its feet hissing loudly. Its tail stood erect, the black fur sticking out like a bottle brush. It spat at him and then lashed out with a vicious swipe that opened three red lines in the back of Rob's outstretched hand.

'Little bastard!' Rob shouted, leaping back. The cat screamed loudly, turned and hurtled out of the room. Rob inspected the damage to his hand. It was already bleeding profusely.

'You'd better wash that?' Maria suggested, barely suppressing a laugh.

'What, in the stream you mean?' Rob suggested. 'Then I can die of infection. Good idea!'

'Don't be so bloody dramatic.' Maria laughed. 'It's just a scratch.'

As the afternoon progressed the twins became more and more enthused with the idea of living there while Rob began to feel alienated to the same degree. To him the old house was nothing more than a pile of bricks waiting to happen. He habitually checked the back of his hand which, despite the application of copious amounts of antiseptic cream from the first aid kit, was now noticeably swollen. God alone knew what that scruffy bastard of a cat had been rummaging through before it had scratched him. He stared out of the cracked kitchen window at the dark woodland still completely unable to understand why Maria was so keen to live here. Maria was a materialist, as everyone who knew her would certainly testify. She insisted on a certain degree of comfort in her life, something that was almost entirely missing in this rank old shit hole.

His attention was grabbed rudely by a squeal of panic from the living room. He ran to investigate.

***

Maria was out at the back garden gate staring at the back of the house. She couldn't figure out why Rob had taken such an instant dislike to the place. Sure, it wasn't what they were used to but it made up for that in so many ways. There was an atmosphere of calm and security for a start, and from the moment you walked in you felt at home, as if you'd lived there all of your life. The girls could feel it, why couldn't Rob?

She'd cleared the weeds from the herb garden and trimmed back the more enthusiastic plants. She sniffed at her chlorophyll stained hands and recognised the dark odour of sage and the refreshing tang of lemon balm. She stretched her aching arms and walked to the back door and after kicking off her gum boots she pushed open the door and stepped inside.

Maria stopped short with a gasp. Rob was labouring furiously with a thick screwdriver trying to lever up a floorboard from the living room floor while both the twins looked on anxiously.

'That bloody cat again!' Rob shouted as he caught sight of her.

'Mummy!' Lulu squealed, 'Greediguts is under the floor!'

'He can't be!' Maria insisted, suddenly reminded of the nightmare that she'd had while asleep in the kitchen, which had featured the same floorboard that Rob was currently tearing up. 'He can't have gotten under there. There's no way in!'

'Well he's found a way.' Rob grunted as he pulled the board free. 'We heard him, and I'm not surprised my hand's so bad if he spends half his bloody time under there!'

Maria stayed by the door, her hands to her face. This was a bit too much of a coincidence. The cat under the floor. Under the very same part of the floor as in her dream. She pushed herself back against the door frame. She knew what was coming next.

'It's not here!' Rob announced lifting his face out of the hole. 'Would you frigging believe it?'

'Put the board back Rob.' Maria told him solemnly. 'It can obviously get out.'

Rob looked into the gap again just to be sure.

'Nope. Definitely not here.' Rob confirmed. 'But there is something else.' He added.

Shit, shit, shit. Maria repeated inwardly.

'There's a glass floor isn't there?' She asked him. Her eyes were closed, already reliving her dream.

'What?' Rob answered. 'A what? No, just this.' He sat back on his heels and presented Maria with a small book. She took it from him. It was very old by the looks of it and had been bound with pale calfskin.

The pages were brown and half rotten at the corners. She opened it carefully. The contents were all hand written and text flowed from left to right but then the book had been turned ninety degrees and the page had then been filled again writing from top to bottom.

There was an inscription inside the cover. Maria read it aloud.

'Livre leFey de l'ombre, seventeen sixty.' Maria whispered. 'French anyone?' She asked.

'Well livre means book,' Rob offered, straining to remember the handful of words that he'd been forced to learn at school. 'and de means of. So at a guess I'd say that it means something like, this book belongs to...'

'But seventeen sixty.' Maria shrugged. 'That makes this book maybe a hundred and fifty years older than this house! How on earth did it get under there?'

'Dunno.' Rob answered. 'Maybe someone just, put it there.'

'Well obviously somebody put it there, bloody Sherlock!' Maria snapped, rolling her eyes. 'What I'm asking is why!'

'Well what's in it?' Rob asked climbing to his feet. The twins gathered around Maria, craning their necks to see.

'It looks like poetry.' Maria stated, flicking through the delicate pages, 'but it's all in French... Oh, wait a minute.' She stopped somewhere in the middle of the book and carefully levered the pages apart. 'Yes, look. This one's in English.' She moved the book back and forth trying to focus on the tiny handwritten words. 'There's no title. It just says that it's by Celine leFey and it's dated eighteen fifty five.'

'Read it out mummy!' Jemma pleaded.

'Not now darling.' Maria answered, 'Maybe later.' Both twins groaned loudly and Rob set about putting the floorboard back in place.

Several hours later, after sharing a plate full of sandwiches, half a packet of chocolate digestives and a large bag of crisps, the twins became lethargic. Maria, tired to her bones after all the gardening, also felt reluctant to move.

'We should stay here for the night.' She suggested. The twins agreed. Rob was most definitely against the idea.

'Where will we sleep?' He asked.

'I've got the kids tent. We can put it up in the garden.'

'It's a play tent.' Rob countered. 'It's not even waterproof, and I think it'll rain before the night's out.' He faked a concerned glance out of the window.

'That's settled then.' Maria announced. 'We'll put it in the living room.'

Rob sagged. His hand was really starting to hurt now. Its constant throbbing interrupted his thoughts. It felt hot and had been swelling at a constant rate ever since that toilet brush of an animal had attacked him. He was unsure now whether or not it needed hospital treatment.

'We should go home tonight Maria.' Rob pressed. 'It's only an hour away and I think I need to get my hand looked at.'

'And you think that me and the kids are going to spend all night in the casualty department because the nasty kitty has scratched your poor little hand?' Maria yawned. 'If you're going to go all soft on us you can take the car to the hospital and come back later. We'll be okay I'm sure.'

'Perhaps I fucking should.' Rob snapped, storming out of the kitchen. He strode to the car, opened the boot and dumped everything out to one side before getting into the car and driving off with a petulant wheel spin.

He drove through the dimness of the woods and the car bounced quickly along the rough pathway. He'd never known Maria to be so bloody inconsiderate. What the hell was it about that crumbling relic of a house that captured her imagination so much?

He put the car's headlights on and could still barely see the path ahead. He was fucked if he was going to live here. It was as if even the trees had it in for him. They seemed to have moved closer together somehow. He peered ahead, into the gloom.

His hand suddenly erupted with pain as if someone had scraped it with a fork. He yelped loudly, taking his hand off the wheel and trying, in the poor light, to see what had made it hurt so much. As he inspected his now bulbous and discoloured hand he caught, in the corner of his eye, a movement ahead of him in the beam of the headlights.

Greediguts was sitting in the middle of the track, nonchalantly licking his paws.

Rob reacted instinctively, wrenching the wheel to one side. He never even saw the huge oak tree and was only marginally aware of bursting face first through the windscreen to his death.

Greediguts finished cleaning his claws and then sauntered off into the woods.

***

Putting up the tent had been a simple matter. The whole thing was just a dome that was held up by flexible carbon fibre rods. It twisted into a hooped shape and fastened in place with Velcro loops.

Maria simply carried it into the living room, threw it into the middle of the floor, pulled open the loops and the tent sprang enthusiastically to attention without further supervision.

She stuffed the kid's sleeping bags to each side and put hers in between them. She used some of the flask water to make the twins each a hot chocolate drink and then used the rest to wash their hands and faces.

As the darkness thickened Maria urged the tired girls into their sleeping bags and then sat between them. Although exhausted the twins' excitement prevented them from settling. Maria decided that now would be a good time to tell them a story. She grabbed the flashlight from a pocket in the wall of the tent and flicked the switch. The light that it gave was a dull yellow.

'Damn!' Maria spat. 'I'm sure I asked Rob to get new batteries for this.' After hitting the torch a few times to fix it and enjoying varying degrees of success, Maria remembered an old box of candles that she'd found while cleaning out the kitchen. She used the remaining available torchlight to seek them out and having managed to light five of them she placed each in a separate cup and positioned them around the edge of the living room. They spluttered shadows into the darkness that loomed over the small tent like the spirit of insanity until the damp wicks had dried through and a warm light drenched the room.

'Well, this is cosy.' Maria giggled, squeezing in between the smiling girls. 'What shall we do now?'

'The poetry book!' Lulu suggested after a brief silence.

'Not sure it's the right thing for sleepy girls.' Maria countered.

'Pleeeeeease!' The twins pleaded together.

Maria sighed dramatically and the twins giggled. She reached for her small leather bag which had been shoved just inside the tent flap. She retrieved the small tattered book and flicked through its worn pages looking for the only entry that was written in English.

The twins snuggled up either side of her.

'There's no title.' Maria began, squinting at the tiny hand written text. 'But it's by someone called Celine leFey and it was written a very long time ago.'

The twins stared up at her with sparkling eyes as Maria began to read...

> *'Tho' gone, not lost, ye lie amidst the grains*
> *of loamy soil as death's cold winter reigns.*
> *A wormed host, A shrunken bag of bones.*
> *A debt thus paid, by want of life atones.*
>
> *The candle bright and full of moon doth plead,*
> *lead me to her as she to me doth lead,*
> *to take the hand that takes mine in return,*
> *The friend that darkness is, is lesson learned.*
>
> *E'en as the sun doth rise from death's decree.*
> *My heart, my loins, my heat, I pledge to thee.*
> *And as my gift of life to death is laid,*
> *will now, to then, and then, to now, be made.'*

Maria rested the book in her lap.

'But what does all that mean mummy?' Lulu asked.

'I'm not sure.' Maria answered. A chill had settled on the house. She shivered slightly.

'Read it again.' Jemma prompted. Maria picked up the book and read the poem out again.

A sudden gust of wind rattled the roof of the house. The trees hissed, the window frames creaked and the candle light flickered madly.

'Again, again.' Lulu begged.

'It's sleep time now.' Maria told her.

'Once more mummy.' Jemma whined. 'Just once more.'

The book felt cold in Maria's hands as she looked at the page. She suddenly felt uncomfortable, but then she looked into Jemma's big blue eyes, so full of expectation. She glanced at Lulu whose pale smooth skin appeared almost waxen in the candle light.

'Once more then.' Maria agreed. 'Then that's it.' She began to read.

She was about halfway through when a loud bang sounded from upstairs. Maria almost jumped through the tent roof.

'Keep going mummy.' Jemma prompted.

Maria continued. Her mouth felt as if it didn't want to move. Each word that she spoke required monumental effort. She felt as if she'd never get there.

'You have to finish it.' Lulu pressed. Her grin now so wide that it seemed impossible. 'All of it. Right to the end.'

As Maria spoke the final line the whole atmosphere seemed to lift. The sensation of relief was almost palpable.

'We need to sleep now.' Jemma smiled dropping her head onto her small pillow.

Maria snuggled down between them, feeling as if she could sleep forever. She felt her tired body relax. Her arms and legs were heavy and the hard floor that she could feel even through her thick sleeping bag felt as welcoming as a feather mattress.

She sighed as if to empty herself completely, and seemed to sink downward, descending slowly into sleep's sweet oblivion as if the earth itself had swallowed her up.

She could hear the remnants of the poem as mental echoes playing through her mind.

'Not a poem...' A small voice said into her ear.

'What?' Maria murmured, barely able to think at all.

'Not a poem...' The bright voice repeated. 'A spell!'

Maria opened her eyes. She was in complete darkness. Only a few narrow slits of pallid light cut through the inky blackness. She tried to lift her head but couldn't move. The realisation that she was somehow underneath the floorboards came too late, as two withered arms reached around her from below and pulled her down into the ground. She screamed in silence as she passed first through the dusty earth and then through the floor of glass into the cold dry cadaver below it.

Maria could feel its frozen limbs; could taste the rot in its soil filled mouth and feel the writhing worms in the sockets of its absent eyes.

Her eyes.

The twins! Maria fought to turn her head, to twist the leathery shrunken neck. They were there with her. She knew this without seeing them. She had chanted the spell for all of them and they would be down here with her, eternally conscious in the cold, damp earth.

***

As the sun rose on the following day Celine LeFey opened her eyes and stared at the roof of the tent. She stretched her long slender arms and gently shook each of her two children awake.

'Come along Lillith.' She urged them. A faint French accent playing on her bright voice. 'Tabitha wake up. We have a world of work to do.'

Lillith and Tabitha sat up and rubbed their eyes.

'The house has changed so much!' Celine gasped, poking her head through the tent flap. 'I'll make us some breakfast and then we'll go through all of these belongings and find out who we are.'

'And will we leave the book behind mother?' Lillith asked, 'When we go?'

'Of course darling.' Celine smiled. 'We have waited, and now it's their turn, and we shall leave them the book. It's the rules. Ah look Tabitha,' Celine laughed as Greediguts ran into the room, 'our old friend is here to greet us.'

Maria heard their ringing laughter and wept in dark silence as Greediguts curled up in front of the empty fireplace purring loudly.

*****

What the butler saw.

The lock almost clunked as it relented to the turn
of a large brass key.

'Good luck with this.' The curator grimaced as he
pushed open the door and handed over the key.

Harry looked into the room. It even smelled old. He
stepped inside, feeling as if he was disturbing
someone.

'No worries.' He smiled. 'A weeks work and it'll be
finished.' He looked around the room as the door
closed softly behind him.

The museum had once been the very grand home
of Mr Earnest Burnley, a woollen mill owner with
several business concerns in the north of England. A
man who had successfully amassed such
phenomenal wealth during the peak of the British
textile industry that his house and the surrounding
grounds were little short of palatial.

There were thirty rooms in the house and like
most of the well to do gentlemen of his time he'd
filled many of them with curious, exotic and for the
most part misunderstood objects from all over the
globe.

Now long since dead, the house had stayed in his
family until his one remaining heir had died
childless. His private collection had then been
transferred into the hands of several trustees who

had maintained the property for approximately the last eighty years.

Eventually and for reasons undisclosed, the property had been donated with its collections intact, to the local council who saw fit to preserve it as it was originally intended, and then to open it to the public.

Initially it had been the usual sort of thing, hardly worth the effort of cataloguing if not for the insurance requirements. Several hundred birds eggs, more than a few from now extinct species, a hundred or so stuffed mammals, birds and reptiles, some unusual fossils and a collection of well kept foreign armaments, mainly swords and knives and a few military uniforms. All in all, nothing but standard curio.

It was when 'the Darkroom' was discovered that things ground to a halt.

The Darkroom was found, and named, by a young woman called Karen Montegue whom, like Harry, had been voluntarily engaged to catalogue the house contents as part of a masters degree course provided by the local university. She had looked at the plans of the house with a view to catering for the displays that would be installed later when she realised that two adjacent rooms on an upstairs floor were somewhat smaller than was suggested by the diagram.

The simple method of tapping on the walls had subsequently uncovered a concealed door, which was unceremoniously revealed by digging away the plasterwork with a pick.

The door was securely locked by a heavy brass deadlock, but the key was soon found. It was one of large bunch that was kept in the council offices. It hadn't been too difficult to spot since all of the others had been accounted for and were labelled with paper tags, whereas the tag on Karen's key held only a question mark.

There were three people present when the door was first opened; Karen, her immediate manager from the Museums department, and a council employee whose entire purpose was to do any heavy lifting.

The house had been wired up for electricity, as one would expect, almost as soon as the new phenomenon had become commercially available. But because this room had been concealed at the time it had not been afforded the same upgrade and since it had no external windows the heavy lifter was immediately dispatched to find several powerful torches.

As soon as the piercing white torchlight sliced into the dusty darkness it became apparent to everyone present exactly why the room had been hidden, because in true B movie horror flick fashion the very first thing that the torch alighted on had been a shrunken head, and Karen, her manager and the heavy lifter had exited the chamber like something from an episode of Scooby Doo.

Her nerve regained, Karen brought in several extension cables and light sources which she positioned just inside the doorway. When she flicked the socket switch, all was laid bare.

A huge wave of occult interest had grown amongst the landed gentry in the mid to late eighteen hundreds and it seemed that Mr Burnley was no outsider in this regard. It seemed in fact that he was more of a progenitor than an observer.

The room housed a collection of objects that all held some occult significance. In the centre of the room there was a circular dark wood table, in the middle of which was a large silver candelabra, a small brass bell, a copy of the Holy Bible and a Ouija board. On the walls were several silk prints and tapestries depicting the 'Otz Chiim', the Cabbalistic Tree of Life, some unrelated sigils drawn from medieval magical texts such as the Lemegeton and various scripts of unknown origin but appearing to strongly resemble incantations from Arabic sorcery.

There were also cabinets, primarily glass fronted, displaying all kinds of paraphernalia of sinister intent, amongst which was the shrunken head that had earlier sent everyone careering from the room, and various potions and powders associated with Haitian Voudoun.

India was represented by a magnificently dark bronze figure of the Hindu Goddess Kali who held, draped over her many arms, presumably authentic silk strangling ropes so often employed by her Thugee cult. Karen also noticed that each object had been individually numbered, with each number being located close to the object on a small label.

The room, in its own way, was already perfect for the purpose of display. It was merely that the content was perhaps a little unsettling. That, and one other thing.

In a far corner was an object so out of place that it screamed aloud of its significance. It could have no other reason for inclusion than that its purchaser believed that it had some power or other.

It was a very early, possibly prototype model of a Mutoscope. These simple machines were commonly found in the amusement arcades that littered the sea fronts of Victorian England and showed 'moving' flick book pictures, often of a risqué nature, as the viewer turned a small handle at the front of the box while staring into the shrouded window. The usual title of the contents was something along the lines of 'What the butler saw...' which gave a clue as to what the customer might experience if he had a penny to put into the slot.

In all honesty Karen had seen worse. She had helped to unwrap an Egyptian mummy in the second year of her degree and had risked catching typhoid in the process. This room, creepy as it was, was not a threat to her, which was a pity because two days later she disappeared and was never seen again.

***

Harry stared at the Mutoscope. He'd already done his homework and he knew that this one wasn't a commercial model. It had an unfinished look about it. The body work would normally be painted with red oxide to protect it from the salt spray in the seafront atmosphere but this one didn't have that embellishment. It was a reasonable conclusion therefore that it was never intended for public use.

Ever since he'd heard about Karen Montegue's disappearance about a year ago he'd been intrigued by the idea of gaining access to this room to see if it had any bearing on the case. He'd had to seriously badger both the council and the university academics to get to where he was now standing.

For a couple of weeks after she was reported missing there had been pictures of Karen in the local rag. He'd pulled all the articles from the microfiche in the local library and printed out the pictures. There was nothing outstanding about her. Nothing in her expression, manner or social habits that said 'I'm a victim. Please kill me.' She had small ringlets permed into her shoulder length strawberry blond hair and she wore a striped turtle necked sweater. That was all he knew about her appearance on the day she went missing.

As he looked around the room he glanced at the round table. Her books were still there. Even the pen that she'd been using. It had rolled into the spine of the large catalogue document in which she was listing all of the room's nefarious objects. It was as if she'd been spirited away somehow. He brushed that idea from his mind. All this occult lark was a load of old shit aimed at prising people's pockets open.

He walked around the room. He stopped to say hello to the shrunken head and to shake one of Kali's many hands. He then decided to get on with the job.

The first thing to do was to play catch up. He unzipped his laptop bag and set up his machine on the table. He'd already installed a self authored database designed to mimic the kind of catalogue that Karen had been using. He cursed to himself as he unfolded the mains cable. The batteries were on their arse and didn't have more than fifteen minutes in them even when fully charged so he needed some mains backup, and herein lay the problem. There was no electricity in this room.

He went off in search of an extension cable to run in from outside. He ended up going off to a local hardware mega store to buy one.

When he'd got back it was lunchtime so he pulled out his packed lunch from the front pocket of his laptop bag and unwrapped the foil from his sandwiches. He sat at the round table feeling in need of something to read while he ate. There was only one book in the room. It sat alone on a low shelf next to the door. Harry got up from his seat and fetched the large leather bound tome back to the table wondering what occult delights it contained. He opened the book and was surprised to see that each page had only a single numbered handwritten paragraph with several signatures at the bottom. It took a while to sink in but he eventually realised that each paragraph was an affidavit, a signed and sworn testament of fact relating to some incident or other.

Another realisation dawned on him and a cold shiver ran down his spine. The paragraph numbers correlated to the numbers that labelled each object in the room.

He glanced over at the shrunken head, which he had only recently given the name Fred.

'Number forty seven.' He murmured to himself flicking through the book. He stopped at paragraph forty seven and learned that this was the head of a British missionary in Haiti who, contrary to his teachings had engaged in untold levels of debauchery and fornication with the local tribeswomen and as a result had been cursed by the witchdoctor to spend eternity pointing out other people of similar habits by biting the fingers from the unfaithful.

Apparently, according to the affidavit, any unfaithful person who attempts to stand the test of truth by putting their fingers in Fred's mouth will have them bitten off, and several eye witnesses had signed the testimonial in support of this.

Harry flicked forward through the pages.

Number fifty one. An Arabian Djinn. A demon reported to reflect the deepest fantasies of anyone who invokes it... not easily controlled... has caused overwhelming lust in several unwary people... locked away for the good of everyone...

'Blah, blah, blah.' Harry chanted, looking at the strange glyph sketched onto the page. He flicked further into the book.

Kali, number eighty six. During the days of the British occupation of India six Thugee practitioners were shot for strangling and robbing British army officers. The silk ropes that they used are the actual ones hanging over the arms of the Kali sculpture. It is reported that in every case the judge who condemned the Thug was killed within twenty four hours of reading his verdict. The really strange thing was that they were all killed by one of the weapons that Kali holds in her six hands. The first one poisoned, the second bludgeoned, the third speared, the fourth stabbed, the fifth strangled and the sixth shot with a bow and arrow. No witnesses saw anyone enter or leave the victim's quarters on any occasion.

So, thought Harry. These weren't just curios. They were genuine objects of provable occult history. This made them tremendously valuable and no less fucking creepy.

He flicked through the pages from front to back as he munched his ham and cheese sandwich. There was no mention of the Mutoscope. He pondered this for a while until the answer hit him.

It was added later. Whatever trustees had been charged with maintaining the estate they had nothing to do with the simple maintenance of a building. They were engaged only with guarding this room and its contents. There must have been a break in communications somewhere down the line and the room must have been forgotten about. Either that or they assumed that it would never be discovered. He looked over to the Mutoscope and saw the cable hanging down from the back of the metal box.

'Of course.' Harry gasped, spraying cheese and ham across the séance table. The flick book inside the machine was backlit with a light bulb. It needed electricity to work, and this room never had any. It must therefore have been stashed away in this room later by whichever trustee had discovered it, and if that person didn't know about the book then its story wouldn't have been entered. He laughed to himself as he swallowed the final bite of his sandwich.

He knew that this was all bullshit. There was no doubt. This was all superstitious, high on drugs, under educated, thick as a brick bullshit. There were no gods, no ghosts, no finger biting heads, no nothing. Harry looked at the plug on the end of the Mutoscope's power cable. It was one of the old round pin types, but not a problem to change. He'd keep the original plug and put it back on once he'd proved to himself that he was right.

That night he pulled the plug from an old portable TV that he'd kept in the loft of his flat. The box had lost its sound years ago and he'd never been bothered to either get it fixed or throw it out. He knew it'd come in handy one day.

He entered the Darkroom the following morning covering a stifled yawn with his hand. He'd slept badly. Maybe the room was getting to him. He'd always been over imaginative. He'd dreamt that some huge maggots had fallen through the ceiling of his bedroom and landed on his quilt. He'd actually jumped out of bed and stood swearing in the darkness trying to brush the bloody things off his naked body. Bizarre!

He pulled the plug and two screwdrivers from his coat pocket and then knelt down in front of the Mutoscope. It was easier than he'd imagined to get the old plug off. There was no stiffness in the screws or brittle fragility in the Bakelite casing. In short time he'd fitted the replacement.

He tugged the Mutoscope across the room, bringing it closer to the end of the extension cable. He plugged it in.

Nothing. The box was deader than Fred the Head. Harry stood looking into the shrouded viewing window which was completely dark. He tried turning the handle. It turned easily enough but it made no difference. Then, suddenly aware of the calibre of fool that he was, he stepped back, slapping himself on the forehead.

Where the hell was he going to get an old penny from?

But then this was a museum after all, and people were always walking in off the street to donate rubbish that they'd found buried in the garden. They were bound to have some. Well, not in this case it seemed. According to Bill Jarvis, the curator, there had been a box somewhere with ten or eleven of them in it but he could no longer find them.

Luckily there was a local council owned stately home that had a few on display in a small cabinet. After much pleading on the telephone he managed to borrow one for a day. How fucking magnanimous of them he'd thought, as he shuffled into his coat. It was a two hour round trip on the bus and he had to sign a receipt for it when he got there.

Late that afternoon he walked into the Darkroom clutching a large Victorian one Penny coin. He'd been playing around with it in his pocket and now his hands stunk of copper.

'Okay.' He whispered to himself after a visual check to make sure that everything was plugged in and ready. 'There is no way that this is going to work.' He pushed his face against the viewing window knowing that the light bulb inside was over a hundred years old and couldn't possibly, possibly, light up. He dropped his penny into the slot.

The bulb lit up.

'No fucking way!' Harry gasped. He reached for the small handle on the front of the box and began to turn it.

The show started with age stained sepia images flicking past his eyes. None of the titles or the ornate framing that would normally be expected, just a single image, a circular glyph of sorts, that danced in the centre of the scope as if begging for attention. It looked oddly familiar.

Then there was a misty blankness that cleared slowly to reveal a dark cobble paved alleyway, narrowly enclosed by the dirty stone buildings of Victorian London. The show moved on at a brisk walking pace. The ground smog swirled in the dim lamplight as if stirred by whoever owned the eyes that the viewer was looking through.

Silently the pace quickened, ducking swiftly down a backstreet carpeted with sodden litter. Discarded cigarette ends floated around rat carcasses in the poorly drained gutter as pooled filthy water splashed aside to the beat of sturdy leather shoes.

He was hunting something. The pace quickened again. Harry felt that he could hear laboured breathing as he ran through the dismal alleys. He ducked left, down the side of a public house, its windows cold and cracked.

And there she was. A young woman plying her trade. Dishevelled, ragged, beaten by misfortune into nothing more than a soon forgotten cheap drunken fuck. A nest for venereal disease and scarred and blinded stillborn babies. Soon she would turn to face him as he approached. She would force an uncertain smile onto her herpes crusted lips in the hope of earning two pennies for a warm supper. How disappointed she would be. How terrified. He hated her. He loathed her.

He drew his knife as she noticed him. As she turned...

Harry threw himself backwards, almost choking. He landed on the hardwood floor, his chest heaved in huge gasps as his mind struggled to recognise reality in favour of what he'd just seen.

He began to laugh although his body felt almost electrically numb.

'Fucking hell!' He chuckled climbing to his feet. He wasn't easily disturbed by horror movies, he'd seen them all. But this was just so far ahead of its time as to be untrue. He was in no doubt now why this machine had been put here. It must have scared the living shit out of people in those days.

Still trembling slightly he went back to the Mutoscope and looked tentatively into the eyepiece.

It was blank. His penny had run out! Harry sagged exasperated. What the hell was he going to do now?

Push it back into the corner and forget about it, his heart said.

His curiosity disagreed. He had a screwdriver in his pocket, he remembered. If he could just get his penny back...

An hour later he held the small metal coin drawer in his hand. He couldn't pick the iron padlock that held it in. He couldn't get to the screws that held the hasp in place. He'd done the unthinkable for a trainee museum curator. He'd damaged it. He'd put the screwdriver stem into the padlock and hit it repeatedly with his shoe until it broke. He felt empty afterwards, but while it was happening it'd felt sort of urgent, necessary even. Like masturbating to internet porn.

The coin drawer held seven worn pennies. Fred the Head stared at him through stitched eyelids as he poured them into his hand and put the drawer back.

Harry put his forehead against the metal shroud of the viewing window and rolled another penny into the slot. The movie flickered into life. The same dancing symbol. The same sepia mist. A different opening scene.

Initially puzzled at how this could happen Harry found the solution in his own mind. The movie frames were interleaved somehow. Each time a penny dropped it must index some kind of ratchet that showed every alternate frame so that you never really knew what you'd get. Very clever. You could hide half a dozen flick movies this way.

A small candlelit room. The dirty cracked widow barely covered by a single tatty curtain. Mould on the damp stained walls. A gaunt, almost emaciated young woman sits on the edge of the sagging single bed. She unbuttons her dirty wool jacket. There's only one button. The rest are lost.

We step forward through anonymous eyes as the candle sputters unexpected brightness into the dank slum. There is no fire in the hearth. It is cold and black. The woman, now opening her yellowing blouse, stares into our eyes, and we see her.

145

'It's not real.' Harry reassures himself, his forehead pressed hard against the cold metal. He stares at her glazed eyes. 'It can't be real.' He turns the crank, fearing to stop.

We rush forward. We draw the knife. The woman screams in silence, raising her bony arms against the flashing blade.

We push her down onto the bed. A trousered knee lands on her angular cheekbone holding her head down. Her fingers claw with brittle splintered nails against our eyes. We push them aside and the knife flashes down into the side of her painfully thin neck. It pulls forward tearing out her throat and splashing black blood up the faded wallpaper.

She still lives as the blade flies again. Digging into her gut at the sternum and ripping through her abdomen to exit at the pubic bone. The frail body spasms softly as the blade is set aside and two hungry hands dip quickly into the wound. They pull back, each full of pale grey offal. They squeeze into fists and dead blood bursts from between the fingers. The hands dip again and again. They tear. They rip. They rend.

And when they are done, exhausted and exhilarated, we step back, away from the eviscerated woman and we leave her in peace. Food for flies.

The Mutoscope darkened with a clunk and Harry stepped back, sickened. He ran his fingers across his forehead. It felt as if it was splitting. There was a thick wheal across it. God knows how hard he must have been pressing against that metal shroud.

He knew what he'd just seen. That was the murder of Mary Kelly through the eyes of Jack the Ripper. He'd seen the case photos, there was no mistaking it. Harry rubbed his head.

But surely Jack the Ripper was an urban myth? Harry had studied each case in depth. Serial killers were something of an obsession with him. Sure there had been some similar killings, all prostitutes, around eighteen eighty nine, but in Whitechapel at that time murder was commonplace and you could ask any ten women off the street after dark and nine of them would to be on the game and the tenth would be lying! The murders attributed to Jack ranged anywhere from a simple cut throat to complete carnage. There was no real pattern as such. It was all media hype and scare mongering engineered to keep the prozzies inside.

The real question was, how did the people who made this film know all the details? The case photos are commonly available on the net now, but at the time they were closely guarded secrets. That's why the brutality intensified, because if you wanted to kill your pregnant hooker girlfriend and then blame it on Jack, you had to go all out in case you missed something.

Harry was a clever man. Everyone said so. So if an idea occurred to him it was probably a good one, although at that moment he'd have given his left testicle to be proven wrong. He sat down at the table and put his aching head in his hands. There was only one reasonable answer. However unreasonable it may be.

It was a fucking snuff movie.

The Ripper murders were snuff movies. Was that possible? There's a market for everything, he reminded himself, even in those days. Yes, it was possible, and all this time the proof had been concealed here in the Darkroom. Hidden way from prying eyes, like the tablecloth hanging down over the ornately carved legs. Cover up the lust and the depravity and it doesn't exist. This Mutoscope was made about eight years before they became commercially available. It must have been commissioned by someone. Someone totally fucking sick.

He had to be sure. He would go to the police. He'd clear it up once and for all. But first he had to be sure.

Harry pulled another coin from his pocket, put his face against the viewer and dropped the penny into the slot. He turned the handle.

The same symbol danced in his vision. The same sepia mist. Another different movie.

A dark alley. It's raining as we approach another young woman. She cowers from the rain. She doesn't want to be there. Of course she doesn't.

There is silent conversation and she smiles falsely. Her wide brimmed hat, trimmed with soddened paper flowers, placed on her strawberry blonde curls at a rakish angle. She nods her agreement and we look from side to side ensuring the emptiness of the alley.

Harry's head hurts again. Is this the same woman? It can't be! There were no special effects in those days. No possible way to fake what he'd seen before. And yet it was. She wore less makeup but it was the same woman.

He hadn't realised until now and his breath caught in his throat. It was Karen Montegue.

'Impossible.' Harry breathed.

She looks cautiously around as she lifts her long skirts, slowly gathering them up in her small hands. We glance downward, catching a glimpse of her white thighs and her soft and downy pubic hair. A nice place. A beautiful moist warm place. The perfect place for a blade.

Shock registers on her young face as the blade thrusts in. We tear upward, pull out the knife and then we slit her throat to stifle her cries.

Too late! She screams loudly as we reach inside and grasp her warm and spongy womb. We tear it out to take with us as we run through the darkness and the rain, police whistles echo in the mist behind us. We run for a long time, and as we run everything becomes clear. Harry is carried along inside the mind of a madman. He feels the thrill of disgust and the euphoria of stunning violence. As he twists and turns through the unending cobbled maze Harry, the unseen passenger, achieves a blinding emotional catharsis.

He likes it here.

He also knows now that none of it is real. There are no flick movies in this Mutoscope. There never were. All that he has seen and experienced has been drawn from the dark recesses of his own id. The dancing symbol that starts the show is the glyph of the Arabian Djinn. The Mutoscope has no power of its own. That's why it wasn't in the book. Someone had taken the genie of this lamp and put it to work, to show every emotionally repressed viewer their own most intimate and powerful desires for the princely sum of a penny each.

A brilliant idea, for who wouldn't want to see them?

But some people's desires are very much darker than others.

Harry had seen Karen Montegue in his mind before. He'd imagined her slender body lying bruised and broken in a remote and desolate place. Half clothed now, beaten, raped, strangled.

It had stirred him and he had been disgusted with himself.

He had studied the detail of the Ripper killings. He had been appalled. He had been moved.

He had been envious.

Eventually we stop in a dark doorway. A gnarled hand grasps the door handle and as the door opens we step back.

No... Not we... I.

I step back. I see the man now. The dark soul who's name is Jack. I stand behind him and he knows that I'm there. He turns slowly.

His face is deathly white. His mouth is a twisted snarl housing crooked stained teeth and a limp pale tongue. His nostrils flare angrily and his eyes are shiny black. Beetle black. I see a thousand tortured souls burning in their blackness and I see myself reflected in those eyes. I see my own face and the dark desire etched into it. He is me, and I am him. I cannot move. He lunges forward...

Jack opened his eyes and stared at the ceiling of the Darkroom. He moved his arms and legs as if feeling them for the first time. He had no idea where he was but he smiled as something urgent burned inside him. It whispered to him over and over again as he walked from the room in search of something sharp. It said...

'So many women, so little time...'

*****

Looking after Granddad.

Billy Giles stepped into the large lounge and looked around him at the plain beige décor and the industrial grade grey carpet. There were several elderly people dotted around the walls in high seat armchairs. Some were chatting, though not necessarily to each other, and one particularly skeletal old woman was staring off into the distance sucking ferociously on her false teeth. The television was uncomfortably loud but no-one else seemed to mind.

'You'll have to get used to the noise.' Orlando informed him. 'Most of them are stone deaf so if you turn it down someone will just turn it up again. They may be old and infirm but they don't take any shit.'

'No.' Billy sniffed. 'I suppose that's my job.'

'Most of it, yes.' Orlando nodded. 'We like to refer to it as starting at the bottom, since that's where you'll spend the majority of your time for the first year.'

'Great.' Billy grimaced.

'Take it from me, we've all been there.' Orlando grinned. 'I've wiped more backsides than I care to remember. There was a time when I thought I'd never manage to wash the smell of shit out of my skin, but you get through it. You'll get your training fully funded by the nursing home but only you can put the work in, so until you're good at something all you get to do with these people is feed one end and wipe the other, okay?'

Orlando led him out of the lounge and down a wide corridor lined with pale grey doors. Beside each door was a small notice board displaying each occupant's name and main carer. They stopped at door number twelve. The notice board had the name Leo McDonald scribbled on it.

'In many ways you got a lucky break when you got Leo.' Orlando told him while pressing the doorbell. 'He's still quite young by our standards so if he shits his pants he mostly has the sense to tell someone about it instead of sitting in it for half a day.' He pressed the bell again. 'On the other hand, he's still strong enough to be a handful and he can become aggressive if he's confused or caught unawares, which is why we make a point of ringing the buzzer and shouting out to let him know we're here.'

Orlando pushed open the door.

'Leo?' He called. 'LEO! Can you hear me?'

'Of course I can hear you, you dumb bastard.' A grating voice replied. 'I just like to wait and see you make a fool of yourself.'

Orlando rolled his eyes and walked into the small apartment. Billy followed on cautiously.

Leo sat in an old arm chair about six feet from a small colour TV which was currently showing a low budget soap opera. He had a half eaten sandwich in one hand and a coffee cup in the other. He wore only a stained, off-white cotton tee-shirt that stretched over his firm round belly, and a pair of equally stained underpants. His legs appeared thin and wasted. His complexion was ruddy. He had the swollen, faintly blue nose of a hard drinker and although mostly bereft of hair he had plenty of silver white stubble on his rounded chin.

'I've brought someone I'd like you to meet.' Orlando said loudly, pulling Billy alongside him. 'His name's Billy. He's your new helper.'

'Don't need any help.' Leo snapped. 'I've never needed any help. Especially from a girly man.'

Orlando and Billy exchanged glances.

'I mean, what's a young man going into nursing for anyway?' Leo asked, not taking his eyes from the TV. 'Unless he likes wiping arses.' He bit into his sandwich. 'Is that why you're here girly?' He shouted toward the TV, firing damp bread and spittle from the corners of his mouth. 'Because you like arses?'

'No... er I...' Billy began.

'What happened to the other one then?' Leo interrupted. 'Where's the other one?'

'I've already told you Leo,' Orlando explained, 'We don't know where Richard is. He just stopped turning up.'

'You never paid him enough.' Leo spat. 'He was always on about that. That's why he tried to steal all my money, because you're all so fucking tight.'

'He didn't try to steal anything Leo.' Orlando sighed. 'He just didn't want to work here anymore.'

'He was okay he was.' Leo insisted. 'Lola would have liked him. You didn't pay him enough.' He finally turned to Billy. 'So how much do they pay the wipers these days?'

'Er, not enough.' Billy answered.

Leo burst out laughing, slopping coffee all over the arm of the chair.

'That's right! He cackled. 'He learns fast this lad. I like him.'

'Good.' Orlando nodded. 'Because you'll be seeing a lot more of him from tomorrow morning.'

'I can wipe my own bloody arse thank you.' Leo countered.

'Well, he can still help out.' Orlando insisted, ushering Billy out of the door.

'He doesn't look like he needs much help.' Billy commented as they walked toward the office.

'He's not what he seems.' Orlando replied. 'He's got a bit of a history. I'll get his file so that you can take it home to read. He loses track of things sometimes. He suddenly thinks that it's twenty years ago and he can't figure out where he is so he gets scared and lashes out.' He handed Billy a thick pale brown folder. 'It's all in here.'

'Who's Lola?' Billy asked.

'What?'

'Back there,' Billy nodded toward the corridor, 'he mentioned someone called Lola. Is that his wife?'

'Probably a pet name for her.' Orlando replied. 'We know that he was married once, but when the authorities brought him in they said he was living alone.'

'The police brought him?' Billy asked with raised eyebrows.

'It's in the file.' Orlando smiled, tapping lightly on the folder.

***

Billy lived with his parents. Not something to brag about for a young man in his mid twenties but they gave him his privacy. He'd been a bit of a late developer. Mainly on account of him having no idea what he wanted to do with his life. He'd left school as soon as possible and he'd had a string of low paid menial positions until the time when he'd been claiming benefits between jobs and a careers advisor had told him to think about what he was good at and try to find a job doing that.

He'd missed out on most of his last year at school because he'd had to look after his old Granddad. Billy's parents were both workers. They worked nine to five and then overtime when it was leading up to a holiday or Christmas, so Billy spent most of his days and nights tending to Granddad until the day that he died. So that was what Billy was good at, looking after Granddad. It had never occurred to him that he could actually get paid for it.

Billy sat on the edge of his bed enjoying the silence. His parents had turned down the TV so as not to disturb him while he was studying. He was about ten pages into Leo's records, which for the most part were about his mental state and the bouts of depression and confusion that he'd been suffering over the past three years. He'd disappeared from the nursing home four times over that period and had inevitably been found at his house, sitting in darkness in the living room, talking to someone called Lola.

Billy had found it strange that Leo still had a house away from the nursing home but there was a letter in with the records from some Christian missionary group or other who actually owned the house and had been renting it to him at very low cost for the past twenty years. Apparently they were happy for him to continue there until he died. It said something about long and exemplary service.

Leo had been diagnosed with some kind of Prion disease. A brain degrading illness similar to Alzheimer's syndrome. There were police reports describing incidents of shoplifting and fits of aggression. He'd tried to run off with a trolley full of meat from a freezer food shop but had been apprehended by the manager as he hurtled down the main street in town throwing frozen chickens at pedestrians. When the police questioned him he'd said that he'd thrown it out because Lola didn't like chicken.

It soon became apparent to everyone that Leo wasn't playing with a full deck. The shop manager decided not to press charges, despite being called a 'pencil necked fucking coward' by Leo as the police carted him off home.

When they arrived at his house the full extent of Leo's problem came to light. The front garden was stacked with rubble and rotting rubbish, in stark contrast to the adjoining terraced properties which had well tended lawns and colourful flower beds. It was almost as if his neighbours where desperately trying to tell him something.

As Leo and two police constables stepped cautiously around the shards of bottle glass on the garden path, one of the neighbours, a fat elderly woman with a blue rinse and a flowery dress, came out onto her doorstep.

'About bloody time!' She squawked. 'You should be taking the silly bugger away, not bringing him back!'

'Fuck off, scrubber!' Leo shouted. The police ushered him on to the front door.

As soon as the door opened the smell hit them. They stepped inside. The narrow hallway was stacked high with old damp newspapers and at some stage in the past ten years or so that he'd been hoarding them all of the vermin for a five mile radius had seen fit to set up home in it. The half eaten, threadbare carpet was almost invisible under a stinking blanket of urine soaked shredded paper and rat droppings. They didn't even bother to hide anymore. There were at least three huge brown rats scurrying along the top of the stacks carrying unidentifiable masses in their constantly twitching mouths.

'Needs a bit of a tidy.' Leo muttered as the two officers squeezed past the stacked newspapers into the living room.

It was even worse than the entrance hall. There were open rubbish bags piled in one corner, many of which had become so overgrown with mould that it was impossible to tell quite what had actually been underneath. The stinking mass ran wick with cockroaches engaged in doing whatever it is that cockroaches do. The window sills were half an inch deep in dead flies and the carpet seemed to squelch underfoot.

Above all of this. Above all of the stench and the decay, were the rats. Hundreds of rats. All dead and tied together in bunches by their tails. They were stacked three feet high on top of the living room table and a further twenty or thirty bunches hung from four inch nails banged into the wall. Some had dried out while others dripped grey fluid onto the carpet from their protruding yellow tongues.

'Mister McDonald.' One officer retched, holding a hand to his mouth. 'You can't live like this.'

'There's no fucking law against it!' Leo shrugged.

But apparently there was a law against it, which was why he'd been sectioned under the mental health act and placed in the care of the local psychiatric hospital while his house had been cleared.

After six weeks in the hospital being treated for skin ulceration due to infected flea bites and every possible parasitic infestation, Leo had been given over into the care of the nursing home under a 'supervised living' order.

Billy flicked further into the paperwork. There were other police reports involving Leo breaking into his own house in the middle of the night and one case of him trying to behead a passer-by with a shovel.

His old vaccination record struck Billy as a bit unusual. Star fever, yellow fever and smallpox were on the list. This would normally suggest military service but there were no records of this. Then it dawned on him. Long and exemplary service to the Christian missionary group. Is that who Leo was? A Christian missionary?

An hour later Billy fell asleep still reading.

Tuesday was his first full day at the home. He remembered what Orlando had told him when he reached Leo's door. He pressed the doorbell and held it in.

Leo answered the door almost immediately.

'What?' He asked.

'It's me mister McDonald.' Billy answered loudly. 'It's Billy.'

'Who?'

'It's Billy. We met yesterday, remember? Shall I get Orlando?'

'What?' Leo asked, leaning toward him.

'Orlando.' Billy grimaced.

'You're not Orlando!' Leo shouted.

'No, I know. I'm... bloody hell.' Billy sagged, exasperated.

Leo burst out laughing.

'Come in you silly fucker.' He cackled. 'I know who you are, I'm not that far gone. Put the kettle on.'

Billy shuffled between the closely placed furniture. The room was tiny but there was a small kitchen off to the right. The sink was stacked with at least three days worth of dishes. Billy filled the electric kettle.

'Where are the cups?' he asked, looking around him.

'In the sink.' Leo grunted. 'Keep washing until you find them.'

'What did your last bloody slave die of?' Billy mumbled as he turned on the taps.

'What?' Leo snapped standing in the kitchen doorway.

'Nothing.' Billy lied.

'Now listen here you little knob rot.' Leo warned. 'I was in the fucking jungle eating spiders to survive when you were still on the tit! If you think you can give me shit then think again. You're the sixth arse wiper I've had in three years and they were all better men than you and I've driven them all out. My shit is your wages so think about it. If not for me you'd be lining up for fucking welfare as we speak.'

'You ate spiders?' Billy asked, slack mouthed.

'Only the big ones.' Leo grunted turning back to his precious arm chair.

Billy finished washing the dishes. He set out the last two mugs for tea and wiped around the surfaces while the kettle re-boiled. Two minutes later he carried a small tray through into the tiny living room.

Leo was fast asleep, knocking out the occasional snort and dribbling from the corner of his mouth.

'Leo.' Billy called softly, placing the tray down on a small table by the chair. 'Mister McDonald.' He leaned over and tapped gently on Leo's shoulder.

Leo screamed and sprang to his feet, flailing his arms and knocking Billy backwards onto the sofa.

'Get it off me!' Leo shouted, tearing at his vest and pulling it over his head. 'For God's sake get it off!' He threw his vest aside and stood panting for breath, finally finding his senses.

Billy half laid there staring at him. He put his hand to his mouth and then checked his fingertips for blood.

'Are you alright?' Billy asked.

'Has it gone?' Leo gasped, wiping tears from his cheeks.

'Er, yes.' Billy replied, hoping to humour him until he'd fully awakened.

'David.' Leo sniffed, reaching down and grasping Billy's clothes. 'David, they're after it again.'

'After what?' Billy asked. 'It's not David mister McDonald, it's Billy. I'm here to...'

'Shhht!' Leo interrupted. 'Don't let anyone know. Just you and me okay?'

'Okay.' Billy nodded. 'I've made us some tea.' He reached over to the table and handed Leo his mug.

'You've always been a good lad David.' Leo sniffed, accepting the mug. 'I couldn't have wished for a better son than you. You're always here when I need...' He stared hard into Billy's eyes for a moment.

'You're not David are you?' He asked quietly.

'No mister McDonald.' Billy answered. 'I'm Billy, your helper.'

Leo collapsed back into the armchair shaking violently.

'He's dead isn't he?' Leo murmured.

'I don't know.' Billy answered.

'Whenever this happens... ' Leo sobbed gently, 'Whenever I get confused... It's like losing him all over again.' He took a drink from his mug and sighed deeply.

Billy reached to the floor, picked up Leo's vest and handed it to him. When Leo lifted it over his head Billy noticed the huge scar just below his left shoulder blade. It looked like a bullet wound but much bigger. The texture of the scar tissue resembled something between a scald and a tearing bite.

'What happened to your back?' Billy asked.

'Mind your own fucking business!' Leo snapped, pulling down his vest.

***

That evening Billy returned to Leo's file. There were several records that were hand written but the handwriting changed periodically. Perhaps Leo had been telling the truth when he said that he'd driven his six previous carers away. Billy resolved not to be the seventh, at the same time telling himself that all the others probably thought that too.

It was always the same story it seemed, inevitably starting with verbal abuse. One female nurse left after approximately six weeks of being referred to only as 'cunt'. If the verbal abuse didn't work then he'd move on to something more physical. Each time claiming either to be confused or that he'd been sneaked up on, or on one occasion that 'the queer bastard deserved it'. He'd also made regular claims

of sexual assault and once demanded that the care
home administrator and an attending police woman
look up his anus for evidence of rape. He'd then
dropped his trousers, pulled his buttocks apart and
farted loudly.

It was almost as if Leo wanted people to hate him,
Billy thought. But why? There were people in the
nursing home in a far more advanced phase of
dementia than Leo and none of them were
aggressive or even antisocial, just confused. What
possible motive could he have for wanting to be
despised by everyone that he met?

Over the next few days, as Leo became accustomed
to Billy coming and going he seemed to become less
apprehensive. Billy took this as a form of acceptance
but occasionally Leo would call him David and then
become angry when Billy corrected him. On one such
occasion he threw a large kitchen knife which
missed Billy's arm by a whisker. Billy had
reprimanded him and Leo had stormed off to the
common room shouting expletives.

Billy, who had been cleaning up the room at the
time, tried to make a note of the outburst in his
notebook. He was duty bound to report all incidents
of aggression in case the nursing home decided to
take the issue further. He cursed aloud as his ball
point pen failed, leaving nothing but a dry
indentation on the page. He searched around for
another pen. There was a large cheap looking
bookcase against one wall. It didn't have many
books on it. It was used as shelving for a few dodgy
pot ornaments and some glass tumblers. In one of
the tumblers were half a dozen ball point pens of
various colours. Billy grabbed one of the pens and
wrote a brief paragraph on his notepad before
putting the pen back. Behind the set of tumblers
Billy noticed a small, pale brown, leather backed
book.

Out of idle curiosity he carefully pulled out the book and, flicking through the hand written pages, he rapidly deduced that this was Leo's diary. He glanced around the room instinctively before beginning to read an entry somewhere in the middle of the book.

... It is a difficult challenge, bringing the word of God to these people, for they only worship that which they respect, and they only respect that which they fear. So, since I have explained to their elders that Our Lord is a loving god and that they have no cause to fear him, they refuse to accept him, preferring instead their own false idol whom they placate with dance and song and almost endless amounts of food...

Billy flicked back toward the front of the book and picked another entry at random.

...savages. They are happy to devour beast and man alike. Indeed I believe that they do not even see a difference between the two. Neither does their hideous god it seems, for they tell many stories of the taking of young men and women deep into the jungle to be left as a sacrifice. I've no idea what these poor souls encounter once left alone to die but it has been said that the very few who somehow survive and manage to return are changed forever by the experience and are given a place of high status in the community until the day they die...

Billy knew it was wrong but he couldn't help himself. He stuffed the small book into his pocket.

Later that night in his room he found the diary again as he changed out of his working clothes. He sat on his bed, flicked on the reading lamp and opened the small book at the beginning.

In the mid sixties and early seventies Leo had been a Christian missionary. One of many European and American do-gooders bent on bringing the word of God to the poor ignorant souls that inhabited the

deepest recesses of Papua New Guinea. On reading
the book it was hard for Billy to imagine who was
actually the most ignorant. The indigenous tribes
people who had never before seen a white man and
had quite understandably mistaken several of them
for food before realising (but never actually
regretting) their mistake, or the missionaries
themselves, who had resolutely marched into an
immensely hostile environment for which they were
profoundly unprepared in the absolute certainty
that they would be protected by the power of their
own prayers.

Leo described with apparent disgust how the
'natives' would all sleep in the same room and how
the adults often fornicated while their own young
children sat watching them. He told of strange
potions that were made from jungle plants that
threw the village shaman into convulsions, after
which he would begin to act like a wild animal and
then vomit on to the ground. He and the elders
would then interpret the swirls of blood and mucous
in the vomit as a means of divination.

His disappointment was evident as he told how
they refused to accept the word of God into their
lives no matter how hard he tried to convince them.
They had their own god. A spidery, voraciously
carnivorous beast that dispensed life and death as it
pleased. They said that it lived in the jungle,
although the thing that they described seemed
hardly credible, being composed of many eyes and
legs and having the capability to eat endlessly. They
believed that it had vomited the entire jungle out of
its dark belly and was now intent on devouring it
again. Leo had dismissed it as some kind of
composite icon. The same as most pre-Christian gods,
it seemed to be made up of a collection of images
that each conveyed related natural laws, in much
the same way that the Egyptian god forms had
arisen.

They had refused God, and Leo had become angry at their unwillingness to save themselves. He had told the elders that their bestial deity was as nothing compared the Lord God who had created not just the jungle but the universe and all that was in it, and who in a single instant could destroy it all, saving only those who believed in him. The elders had called him a child and told him to come back when he was a man. Leo had vowed to do just that.

For four years he lived with them. Shunning even his fellow missionaries in favour of living amongst those he termed 'the ignorant'. He slept alongside them, ate what they ate and took part in their often bizarre paganistic festivals.

When he became able to survive alone in the jungle the elders prepared a rite of passage for him. They took him from the village, walking him through the night until the reached a tiny clearing where a small fire was lit and a paste prepared from various plants. Leo was made to eat half of the paste while the remaining half was spread on his back on two points where the shaman had said were weak spots that would allow evil spirits to enter his soul. The paste made him light headed and his body felt numb, as if it weren't quite his anymore. Another man brought forth a set of wooden chisels and a pot of black paste and tattooed deeply into his back a strange insect like glyph with cavernous jaws and thin spindly legs.

'This is our god.' The shaman grinned through stained and broken teeth. 'He guards the windows to your soul now. No spirit dares to pass him.'

They dragged him to his feet and made him walk on through the darkness, deeper into the jungle. The drug he'd ingested made his head spin and he stopped frequently to vomit until its effect lessened. Each time he retched the shaman would spend several minutes inspecting the bitter mix of half digested food and mucous by torchlight. Sometimes he would nod and smile, other times he would appear confused but always they struggled onward.

When they finally stopped amid towering, vine ridden trees and twisted fern like undergrowth, Leo fell to his knees exhausted. His back burned and bled ink stained scarlet rivulets that ran down to his ankles.

'And now that I've become a man,' Leo gasped, 'will you listen?'

'No.' The shaman grinned, shaking his head. 'Now that you're a man I will show you.' He gripped Leo under the arms and lifted him up, pushing him face first against a tall narrow tree. The other man tied a thin vine to one of Leo's wrists, passed it around the tree and then tied it to the other wrist, holding him firm. Leo didn't have the strength to resist and the rough bark dug into his skin preventing him from sliding down the trunk.

'Ours is the god of birth and death.' The shaman spat. 'You will leave here by one path or the other.' He and his accomplice walked calmly into the dense jungle, leaving Leo alone in the darkness...

***

The next morning as Billy walked along the corridor to Leo's room, Orlando called him back to the office. When he walked in Orlando closed the door.

'I see you got off to an early start then.' Orlando grimaced.

'What?' Billy asked.

'Leo's been in here for over an hour this morning ranting about how you've stolen something from his room.'

'I... I don't know what he's on about.' Billy stammered. He could feel his face reddening. He wasn't a good liar and this was going to be the shortest career in history. 'What has he said is missing?'

'He hasn't.' Orlando shrugged. 'Which makes me think that he may be just bullshitting like he has with all the others. It's just that he normally waits a month or two before he starts with the false allegations. Are you getting on alright?'

'I thought we were.' Billy sighed. 'Maybe he doesn't like me after all.'

'We need to confront him about it.' Orlando suggested. 'We're obliged to take these things seriously but it won't be the first time he's made things up just to get some attention.'

Both men walked down the corridor to Leo's room. Billy's mind raced. How the hell was he going to get out of this? It was just a small diary, not the bloody crown jewels! And he'd intended to bring it back anyway. He resolved to deny everything and then sneak it back when he got the chance. Maybe he could convince Orlando, if not Leo himself, that it had simply been misplaced.

Orlando knocked loudly on the door and then softly pushed it open.

'Leo.' He called. 'Billy's here.' Both men inched into the room.

Leo seemed to spring from nowhere. He grabbed Billy by the throat and slammed his head back against the wall. Orlando wrapped his arms around Leo's chest from behind and tried to pull him off but Leo was a heavy man, and Billy, who weighed about a hundred and thirty pounds wet through and was still dazed from the impact, was of no help.

'Where is it you little bastard?' Leo screamed into Billy's face. 'What've you done with it?'

Orlando heaved him backwards and both of them collapsed onto the sofa. Billy slid down the wall clutching his throat. Leo lashed out at him with his foot.

'Where is it?' He screamed.

'What?' Billy moaned. 'I haven't got anything of...'

'You've fucking spent it all. You greedy little shit!' Leo interrupted kicking out at him again.

'I... What?' Billy asked.

'You know!' Leo shouted. 'You fucking know!' He turned to Orlando. 'He's found my cash tin. He's stolen all my money! I'll kill the little bastard!' He lunged into the kitchen and pulled open the cutlery drawer.

'Billy get out!' Orlando shouted. Billy leapt to his feet and set off down the corridor. 'Go to the office and lock the door behind you.' Orlando called after him. 'Then call the police.'

By the time Leo came back, scarlet faced and carving knife in hand, Billy was nowhere to be seen.

'There's no money Leo.' Orlando told him calmly. 'Your pension goes into the bank. Billy can't get it there.'

Leo looked momentarily blank.

'If you carry on like this they'll put you back in the hospital Leo. You know that.' Orlando continued. 'Have you taken your medication today?'

'Don't fucking need it.' Leo grunted.

'Put the knife down Leo and take your pills. Then you'll see. I'm not lying to you Leo. If you hurt Billy it'll be back to Saint Lukes, or maybe worse.'

'... isn't anything fucking worse.' Leo mumbled, throwing the knife aside.

In the office Billy was sitting by the telephone trying to make up an excuse for not calling the police. Leo had accused him of taking money, which meant that the police would be bound to make some form of investigation however cursory, and if they found the diary well, that would still undermine his credibility.

There was a knock at the office door.

'Billy, it's me.' Orlando called through the frosted glass panel.

Billy unlocked the door and let him in.

'It's okay.' Orlando sighed. 'He'd forgotten to take his medication. Give him an hour and he'll have forgotten all about it. You should call the police back and tell them it was a false alarm.'

'I didn't call them.' Billy answered, rubbing his neck. It felt stiff and bruised where Leo had squeezed it. Orlando stared at him.

'Billy are you hiding something?' He asked.

'No!' Billy insisted. 'No, not at all. I just... It's about trust isn't it? I have to get him to trust me or we'll never get on and if I keep running to the coppers every time we have an argument...'

'An argument?' Orlando interrupted with raised eyebrows. 'If I hadn't been there he may have done you a serious injury. You can't take this lightly.'

'I'm okay, honest.' Billy assured him. 'If it ever happens again I'll report him, but not this time. Everybody deserves a second chance.'

Orlando just stared at him for a while.

'Well, I wish we had more like you.' He shrugged finally.

***

... it's been a while since I've written anything in here but I have to, because if I don't I think I'll lose it. I think I may forget all that I've experienced in this place and believe it all a bizarre dream. Not because it is untrue in any way, or that I've lost my mind, but because the things that I've seen and done have been the stuff of nightmares, and nightmares are by their nature, forgotten quickly...

... I remained hung against that tree for three nights with that thin but wiry vine that held my wrists digging so painfully into my skin that I could barely move to free myself without retching with the agony of it.

The first night I spent under the influence of the shaman's drugs. Assailed by fitful vivid dreams of nattering demons screaming obscenities and snapping at my skin with broken teeth. The following day was spent in fear that the slightest of sounds heralded one of the deep jungle's many predators while I in a much weakened state and being tied in this manner would be completely defenceless against it.

By early the second night I was praying constantly for God's help and sobbing profusely as I became ever weaker and less able to stand. I swear with God as my witness that the only thing that held me upright was the bark of that despicable tree that hooked me by the skin of my chest and belly.

As the sun set that day I heard a loud buzzing sound that filled the air around me. I shook my head thinking myself deranged as every other sound was drowned out. Then the sky darkened quickly, every inch of it filled by the densest cloud of mosquitoes that I'd ever seen. Each one of the disease carrying, blood ravenous insects was more than an inch long. I swear that I could feel the breeze from their countless wings as they alighted by the thousand on my naked body. I felt them pierce my already swollen skin and I cried aloud.

For several hours the mosquitoes came and went. Each taking its fill of my life blood and depositing all manner of parasite and infectious disease in return. As morning broke they departed, leaving the flesh of my back and legs sore and burning in the wet heat. I knew little of the following day. I remember fading in and out of consciousness and hearing my parched throat crying feebly for help. I remember dreaming of home between bouts of agonised lucidity and wondering which was real.

On the third evening the mosquitoes came again and I thought that surely this time they would drain me of every last drop and leave me dead, still hanging from the tree trunk by my own grey flesh. As they descended on me like the angel of death, penetrating my inflamed skin with a thousand needle sharp prosbosces, I had the good fortune to lose consciousness.

By the grace of God I awoke some time later to find the mosquitoes gone. I felt a strange form of clarity then and my pain was greatly relieved. I'd heard it said that when death is close all pain is washed away and I feel no guilt in saying that I welcomed the end. Even though I'm damned to hell for thinking it, I was happy by then to give up my body and to leave it as carrion for whatever beast passed by.

John Vault

I began to recite my favourite psalms which I found that I could easily remember despite my severely weakened state. I sung hymns and chanted prayers in the hope that my soul would be carried aloft on them.

It was then that the angel came, although it may have been my own delusion telling me so, for it started with an overpowering aroma that pervaded everything. An astonishing fragrance that drifted in from nowhere with a honey sweetness that at once cleared my mind and eased my pain. It filled me with strength and energy and even hope itself seemed reborn.

The heavenly scent moved. Slowly, as if viscous, I felt it drawing me on. I could feel with my whole being that I must follow it. Follow it or be doomed to stay there until my bones, whitened by the ravening mouths of a million insects, finally fell into a heap at the base of this tree.

I breathed deeply and the fragrance filled my soul with fire. I gathered what strength I had, balled my fists and pulled against the vines that held me. I swear that I felt the skin of my wrists part as the vines cut in, but I felt no pain. I pulled and hung against their wiry grip until they seemed to cut into the bone itself. I leaned back and screamed, hanging all of my weight against the vines and by God's grace one of them finally snapped, hurling me backwards to the ground.

Invigorated by my success and drawing huge breaths of the glorious aroma I climbed unsteadily to my feet. My senses were fully alert and my mind enjoyed a degree of clarity that I have never experienced either before or since. I followed the angel as it guided me on through the dense jungle for perhaps a half an hour when I found myself at the entrance to a burrow of some kind. The entrance was large. Large enough for a grown man to enter with little more than a stoop. There was no doubt that this was where the smell was originating. As I looked inside I could see that the walls of the burrow were lined with a strange mucous like liquid. I dipped a finger into the liquid and touched it to the tip of my swollen dry tongue.

All at once my whole being was filled with fire and strength. I can barely describe the effect that it had on me. I lapped greedily at the sweet mucous and ignoring the dirt and stones that came with it I swallowed my fill.

Uncle John's Bedtime Tales

As I sat resting by the burrow entrance my mind suddenly became awash with the most intense sensations. The tree canopy high above me that hissed constantly, buffeted by the warm air above, seemed to reverberate like a vast ocean. The damp, moss covered rock on which I sat felt as soft and comforting as a feather pillow and the bird song that had drilled itself incessantly into my mind before now appeared to me as a symphony, and not just of sound but of colour. Colour almost as vivid as the plumage of the very birds that made it.

I sat staring around myself and laughing at my new perspective. My whole world had melted into one glorious mingled sensation, and in that mixture, or rather from it, I heard a voice.

The voice was as mellifluous as any that I've ever heard. It seemed to me to be the voice from which all other sounds came. I thought it the voice of God. It called to me and I followed it.

I bowed my head and entered the cool darkness of the burrow. How deep it went I cannot be sure but in the ten or so minutes that I spent following that serene voice, stumbling over rock and root in the darkness, I only ever walked deeper into the earth.

All at once the ground beneath me seemed to fall away. I slid helplessly downward, coming to rest in the blackness. The voice had gone, leaving me alone in a cold dark void with only the sound of my panicked breathing that resonated against the walls around me. I climbed to my knees. Unable in the darkness to find my way back, I reached out with my hands and began to inch forward in the hope of finding my bearings.

There was a sound then. A swishing sound, as of something moving quickly, almost whip like, in the still air. I stumbled forward as I turned my head to hear it again and my face brushed against something. I can't be sure what it was but it was hard and covered with hairs that were thicker than needles. They tore the flesh of my face and drew an agonised gasp from me.

I looked up, expecting nothing more than inky blackness but I saw something there that I have no words to describe. I saw a mass of faintly glowing eyes bunched thickly around a beak like mouth filled with row upon row of triangular teeth. A hallucination perhaps? Brought on by panic and imagination? I'm not sure anymore. All I know is that I lost consciousness then and awoke again at the entrance to the burrow in the early evening with no memory of making the journey back.

I clambered to my feet which although swollen and bruised gave me no discomfort. My dearest wish then was to find my way back to the village and to safety. I began to walk without a clue as to the right direction. All I know is that the jungle itself seemed to show me the way, clearing a path before me as I walked. I felt almost invincible as first I walked and then ran through the thick growth. I could hear everything that went on around me as if connected in some way to every living thing. After two hours I stopped to rest and came upon a huge spider sitting on the root of a tree whereupon I scooped it up and stuffed it into my mouth. I remember giggling as its spindly legs that stuck out from between my clamped lips wriggled and flicked against my chin in an effort to free it. I remember its large hairy abdomen bursting between my teeth and drinking down the slush from its fleshy gut.

I moved on, and after several more hours I heard the first faint voices from the village cutting through the jungle.

I have to say that despite the impossibility of my return, the shaman who had left me there to die almost looked as though he expected to see me. I put this down to nothing more than bravado on his part because thereafter he treated me with a level of respect that was nothing short of reverential. He took me into his home and inspected by body from end to end, tending to all of my wounds with great attention.

It took perhaps two weeks to recover and apart from a mild swelling in two tattooed areas of my back that still remained I felt as good as I ever have.

On the fifteenth morning after my return I awoke to find the entire village deserted. Each small mud house that had formerly sheltered several extended families was now empty and stripped of anything of use.

I have no idea why they have left me behind but I think that it was their intention to do so and as such, my chances of finding them again are slim.

As I write these words I feel a strong urge to rejoin my companions at the mission and perhaps even to return home. What I have learned from this I am unsure but I know that my faith in God is shaken. I know that He could have saved me this ordeal and that He chose not to, and yet I am alive against all odds and perhaps that is His doing...

Billy put down the diary and lay on his bed by the glow of his bedside light. The words that he'd read, if true, were the words of an articulate and gentle soul and Leo couldn't possibly have written them. If he had, then what had happened between then and now to turn him into the brutish character that he had become?

The following morning Billy arrived at the Nursing home and headed straight to Orlando's office. He found him sitting at his desk, surrounded by paperwork and several empty coffee cups.

'Do you think I should drop in on Leo today?' Billy asked.

'You can try.' Orlando sighed. 'But don't be surprised if he doesn't want you around him. If his drugs are working he's going to be very embarrassed about what happened yesterday and he's not the apologetic type so he may disguise it behind aggression.'

'Nothing new there then.' Billy shrugged.

'Just make sure you're wearing this.' Orlando smiled pulling his hand from his desk drawer. He threw Billy a long string loop with a small black box attached. In the middle of the box was a large orange button. 'Hang it around your neck and if you feel threatened at any time just press the button. All of the alarms will go off and we'll have someone there in a matter of seconds okay?'

Billy set off down the corridor to Leo's room. He pushed the doorbell button and waited. No-one answered. He pushed the button again and then banged on the door with his fist.

'LEO!' Billy shouted, taking no chances. 'LEO. It's me Billy.' Again there was no response. Tentatively Billy turned the door handle and pushed it open. 'Leo are you in here?' He called.

There was a soft sobbing sound coming from the living room. Billy reached into the top pocket of his smock and grasping the panic button firmly, he stepped inside.

Leo was sitting in his chair. He was hunched over and his body was shaking. When Billy walked in Leo looked up at him. His eyes were reddened and tearful.

'I'm sorry Billy.' Leo moaned. 'For what happened yesterday. I just don't know where the fuck I am most of the time these days. It's been getting worse these past six months or so. I try to keep it together I really do, but it's so hard.' Billy just stared at him, still gripping the panic button. Leo saw the string around Billy's neck and nodded his recognition of it.

'So you're scared as well eh?' Leo asked.

'Just not taking any more chances that's all.' Billy answered.

'Just as well.' Leo nodded. 'I reckon I need to be back at the loony bin after all.'

'Not yet Leo.' Billy sniffed. 'You just have to take the tablets that's all. Have you taken them today?'

'Yes.' Leo replied. 'Could do with a nice cup of tea to wash them down though eh?'

Billy didn't move.

'Just one more chance?' Leo sniffed.

Billy nodded and turned for the kitchen.

'There's a good lad.' Leo half smiled.

The kitchen was already clean. Billy assumed that Leo had kept it so by way of an apology. He filled the kettle. He pulled out the tea tray and set it with two mugs with a teabag in each. Milk and two spoons of sugar, that's how they both liked it. When the kettle boiled, Billy filled the cups and added the milk before gathering up the tray and heading for the doorway.

'Hey Leo.' Billy called out. 'Where's those chocolate biscu...'

He had no time to respond as Leo hit him across the side of the head with a thick wooden rolling pin, lifted the tray full of boiling liquid into Billy's face and then pushed him with it. Leo then threw him up against the fridge and butted him in the nose before ramming a bony knee into his testicles.

Billy slid down the fridge door and Leo landed another knee in his face. All thought of pressing the panic button was gone as Billy lapsed into darkness.

'...David.' Leo called softly. 'David can you hear me?'

Billy groaned softly as consciousness returned and along with it the pain of his scalded face and broken nose. He ran his tongue across his split and swollen lips and found that one of his upper front teeth was gone.

'David.' Leo called again.

Billy didn't move. He became aware that he was now sitting on the sofa and that he needed medical attention if he wasn't going to be scarred for life. His best plan then was to play along with Leo's delusion until he could engineer an opportunity to escape. He opened his eyes slightly. The lanyard that held the panic button was gone. He lifted his head slowly.

'I took the box thing away.' Leo informed him casually. 'They were using it to control you. But they can't do that any more so we can talk freely.'

'What?' Billy mumbled through the pain in his mouth, suddenly realising the true depth of Leo's delusion.

'David.' Leo called, shaking Billy by the shoulder. 'Try to stay with me son. They're after it again. We have to move it before it's found.'

'Yes.' Billy nodded, feeling as if his face was about to burst open. 'We'll move it. Let me go and I'll do it now.'

'David wake up!' Leo slapped him hard across the face. Billy's nose, already split wide across the bridge splattered blood up the living room wall almost four feet away. He shrieked loudly. It was like being burned all over again. 'I've moved it but it's not safe. I move it every time I go home. They think all my pension's in the bank so that they can take it when I die but it isn't. I run off every six months and draw it all out. It's in a plastic bag at home under the floorboards in the front room with the rest of my savings. Forty thousand pounds. You have to move it David. You're the only one I trust.'

Billy was sobbing now. The pain in his face was more severe than anything he'd ever endured in his life. He wasn't a tough guy, but under the same circumstances he doubted that anyone would be.

'Under the floorboards.' Billy repeated, sniffing loudly. 'In the living room.'

'That's right.' Leo nodded frantically. 'Here, take this.' He gave Billy the panic button. 'But don't put it around your neck. If you do you're back in their control and we're lost. Do you understand?'

Billy nodded softly.

'Good.' Leo smiled lifting Billy by the arm and setting him unsteadily on his feet. 'Go on then. There's a good lad.'

Billy shuffled out of Leo's apartment and then gathering all of his strength he ran down the corridor to the office.

***

He'd spent six hours in the local casualty department, although admittedly a great deal of that time had been spent waiting for this or that doctor to see him.

They'd looked at the burns and thankfully they were unlikely to scar but they'd given him lots of special cream to apply every few hours to aid the healing process. The emergency dentist had x-rayed his jaw and announced that his remaining teeth were undamaged but that since Billy hadn't had the presence of mind to find the missing tooth and bring it along with him in a cup of cold milk he was unable to save that one. Billy wasn't even aware that they could be put back in.

His nose had been set and stitched and he had a splint on it held in place with large sticking plasters. Both his eyes were now blackened and swollen and he was up in his room feeling thoroughly miserable. At least he'd been given time off work to recover. It was the least that they could do. Orlando had looked utterly shocked when Billy had burst into his office. The police had been called and would be turning up tomorrow to take a statement.

Billy was toying with the idea of pressing charges against Leo for assault. He should have but he knew that somewhere along the line Leo would end up getting off because regardless of the damage done he was plainly of unsound mind and therefore not responsible for his actions.

He could have pressed for compensation from the nursing home for not protecting him properly, but he liked Orlando and he hadn't worked there very long so it could be his fault as much as theirs and he didn't want to tarnish his future prospects.

He rolled this logic around in his mind until his head hurt but despite his best efforts there was something that he just couldn't wipe away. The mind sometimes just doesn't agree with the heart, and in his heart Billy was absolutely certain of something.

He now hated Leo McDonald more than anything in the world.

For the next week his dreams were plagued with symbolic, and often not symbolic, re-enactments of Leo's attack on him. He awoke in the night choked with fear having relived the boiling tea being thrown into his face. His heart wanted revenge. His mind searched for an answer.

When the swelling around his eyes had subsided enough to allow him to read effectively and once the pain in his severely bruised testicles had backed off enough to allow him to stay in the same position comfortably, he picked up Leo's diary again. He opened the small book, and with bile rising in his throat, he began to read.

... reassuring to be in a hospital that's actually clean and where people aren't constantly fighting for resources. The doctors here are very clever. They should be able to figure out why the lumps on my back are still swelling. They've tried all of the antibiotics they have and none of them have worked. Steroids made matters worse. The only thing that they can come up with is that the ink that the shaman used to make these foul tattoos had some kind of toxin in it and unless they can figure out what it is they'll have to cut them both out before I get septicaemia...

... The lumps are huge now and seem to be getting bigger by the hour. The surgeon says that I'm down for the operation tomorrow morning. He's going to have to take skin from by legs and buttocks to cover the gaps but he says that the infection is very limited and so I should be okay...

... When I came round from the anaesthetic my upper back felt as if it were on fire. The swelling that was on my left shoulder blade is gone. The other swelling, above my right kidney, is still there. I've been placed in a side room away from the other patients and I have to wait for the

surgeon to come and explain why he stopped half way through. None of the nurses will talk to me about it...

... The surgeon came in to see me this morning. His hand is bandaged up. He says that he's never seen anything like this in his life and nor has any other surgeon or doctor of tropical medicine that he's been able to get in touch with. Apparently he made an incision around the edge of the tattoo and it moved! The whole lump just started writhing about inside. He cut deeply into the middle and poked around and then one of the theatre nurses screamed and this white thing with half a dozen legs started heaving its way out of the hole. Everyone jumped back as it dragged itself out and tried to get away. The surgeon caught it and it bit one of his fingers off! The anaesthetist grabbed it with a pair of forceps and pushed it into a plastic bucket. They drowned it in ethanol. It's been sent away to be identified...

... I just want to escape. Everyone's watching me like I'm some kind of bloody criminal! I haven't done anything. None of this shit is my fault. How would they like it if they had something living inside them? I hear the other one as it gets bigger. It's like we're connected. It knows that its brother is dead and I feel its pain. This one, the female, is terrified. It begs me to protect it and I share in its distress. I have to get away...

... It's all clear to me now. It's as the shaman said, ours is the god of birth and death and only one path may be taken. The creature in the hole spared my life and in return I have to foster its children like hideous cuckoos. I've failed one of them, but not the second. I'll get out of this place if it's the last thing I do...

... If I don't survive and if anyone finds this book I want them to know that I'm sorry. Sorry for strangling that poor nurse and stealing her security pass. Sorry for running away and endangering lord knows who by giving birth to this creature. Sorry for everything...

John Vault

... been here for three days now. A small lodging house in the middle of nowhere. They don't disturb me. I think that I disturb them though. This lump on my back is almost eighteen inches in diameter and sticks out like a sack of coal under my coat. She's getting bigger. She speaks to me constantly now. It's almost time...

... There was very little pain, but so much blood. I bought ten or eleven bed sheets from the local charity shop and spread them over a polythene sheet to protect the carpets. The first significant movement happened at around three in the morning. It was hard to describe. Like having my skin tugged but from the inside. Lots of fat over the kidneys. Lots to dig through.

I started sweating profusely at around four thirty. My whole body felt feverish. She had scraped most of the fat away and was almost visible now under the skin. I used a shaving mirror to watch her work. Desperate to be free. At five eleven the pain really took off. I had to bite onto a rolled up towel to stifle my screams. In the end I took a straight razor and broke the skin myself.

She pulled herself from me drenched in blood and clothed in strings of yellow fat. She heaved herself onto the floor and sat there exhausted. I reached for a towel and threw it over her before tending to my wound. The hole was thankfully no more than four inches across and strangely painless. I was able to clean and stitch it quickly. I went back to her and dried her off. She is an alarming creature. Six legged, deathly white and brittle looking, she mewls and cries like a kitten but as far as I can see she is without eyes or hair, and is not dangerous. She is hungry though. She eats a lot and is almost entirely carnivorous. Luckily I had prepared for this by buying samples of everything imaginable from the local shop. I really had no idea what to expect...

... Her eyes are open and there seem to be more of them every day. She has about thirty so far, all creamy white. Her pink skin is hardening and becoming darker. She likes to be stroked but I think that the rapidly growing hairs on

her legs and body will make it uncomfortable to do so for much longer...

...We move on. I transport her in a medium sized suitcase. She prefers the darkness now. It's in her nature. She still eats ravenously and we still talk without speaking. She is of high intelligence and has profound emotions...

... I had expected her appetite to level off at some stage but it hasn't. No matter what I offer her she cries for more. I don't know how to satisfy her hunger...

... Too much. She screams too much. All through the day and night. No-one else can hear her. I'm tied to her and her to me. I am in total despair. I feel her hunger as if it were my own. Her screams will drive me mad...

... given up on God. There is no hope for me now. I'm doomed to hell. For four nights she called out. Screaming, crying, begging for food. I felt that my brain would explode. I went out. It makes no difference, the distance between us. She is with me always. A middle aged woman sits alone in a bar. I buy her drinks. She is flattered by my attention. I drug her drink. Gently, not too much. Just enough. We get home and I take off her clothes. She giggles in the semi-darkness. I leave the room. My hungry daughter hides under the bed. Not even a scream...

... Is this how it will be then? Life after life? And is this me? Doomed to play murderous servant to her endless lust for flesh? Tonight I told her, enough. She is large now, and strong. Strong enough to find her own food. I will take her somewhere. Somewhere dark where she can hunt for herself. She lunges out from the darkness under the bed and screams inside my heart. If I do not feed her she will feed on me...

... I live in fear now. Under constant threat. She taunts my mind with her lust for food. She plays images of her frenzied feeding in my minds eye. I am disgusted and filled with loathing and fear. I live from hour to hour with the

dread that the next poor soul she devours will be me. I am appalled at my own cowardice...

Billy threw the small book aside. There was little doubt in his mind now that Leo was insane. That last entry was made eight years ago. Who knows how much further he'd degraded mentally since then. What bothered Billy was not that Leo imagined that his primitive tattoos had somehow come to life, that was obviously delusion, but that some other parts of the story may be true. Leo was violent. Billy had first hand evidence of that. But had he, as his diary suggested, actually been killing people with the notion that he was doing it to feed this fictional creature? One thing was for sure. He wasn't going anywhere near Leo McDonald ever again.

Another idea occurred to him as he lay there. What if Leo really had all that money hidden in the house? He had no real need for money where he was and Orlando had already said that he got a regular pension. Add the fact that Leo only ever told Billy where the money was when he felt sure that he was talking to his lost son David and there was a strong possibility that Leo may be telling the truth.

Billy wasn't naturally dishonest but he knew he was owed something. He could go and check. He knew the address and it wasn't far away, and if the cash was there and he took some of it Leo could rant and rave as much as he liked because nobody believed that he had the cash in the first place.

Leo McDonald owed him, big time.

That night Billy had his first restful night for nine days.

He waited a further three days before going to Leo's house although he thought of little else during that time. Each time he winced in pain from his injuries his hatred intensified. Every time the thin wisps of steam rising from his teacup stung the scald marks on his face his gut felt like it had been cracked with a whip.

He stepped off the bus into the twilight rain and walked along the road to the end of Stepney Street. Leo lived at number forty five.

Billy didn't want to go straight down the front path because it was too exposed and being a terraced house there was no room down the sides of the house to get around to the back. The backs of the houses came out into a small alleyway that ran parallel to the main street. Billy turned off down the alley and walked back and forth a few times looking for a means of entry. There wasn't anything immediately visible but then Billy wasn't an experienced burglar. He did know one trick however. The small ventilation windows had old, swinging arm latches that were poorly fitted and had to be forced onto the pegs. Sometimes, if you bang on the window frame a few times the arm just springs off the pegs and the window opens. He'd see his father perform that very trick on their own house when he was a kid and they'd lost the door key while out on a day trip.

Billy looked around again to make sure he wasn't being watched before opening the back gate. Once into the back yard he was pretty much out of sight. He had a glance through the kitchen window. The place looked uninhabited apart from a plate and a bowl on one shelf and a small electric kettle that hinted at the possibility that someone may actually live there.

Feeling lucky, he tried the door. It was locked. He tried banging on the small window frame with his fist. The latch was loosely fitted and it jumped when he hit it, but after several attempts he gave up. If he'd kept on going eventually one of the neighbours would have investigated all the noise.

Billy knew how people thought. The average man, upon having a new idea, inevitably imagines that he's the only one who's ever thought of it. So if there was a spare key hidden anywhere around for emergencies, it was very likely to be hidden where Billy would have hidden it.

He looked around for clues. There was an entirely out of place red brick on the path next to the door. Billy turned it over. No luck. There were several cracked flagstones which Billy also turned over with similar results. He pulled aside the metal dustbin. Nothing. He was going to have to use force.

There was a very small wooden tool shed. The roof was okay but there were several slats missing from the front section and the whole thing looked like it wouldn't tolerate being leaned against. He pulled open the flimsy panelled door and, bowing his head, he stepped inside.

Virtually anything would have been worth a go. A big screwdriver, or even a shovel. Just something to force a small window. There was nothing except a few scraps of wood, some potting mix and a few cracked flower pots. He turned to leave and almost gasped aloud. On the door frame was a key hanging from a small nail. No way. Billy exclaimed inwardly.

He took the key and pushed it into the back door lock, grimacing as he tried to turn it with little expectation of success.

The lock turned smoothly and the door opened.

Billy stepped inside. The kitchen smelled of stale water, like a leaky washing machine. There were all kinds of strange stains up the walls and scrape marks on the linoleum flooring as if some one had been shovelling from it. He checked all of the cupboards. Empty, except for the odd spider carcass. The drawers were much the same save for a few knives, forks and spoons.

He wandered into the living room. The smell in here was an unpleasant but bearable mix of chlorine and damp rot. God alone knew what the council cleaners had had to use to kill all of the wildlife in this place. There were large, spring loaded traps positioned strategically in each corner, one of which had successfully caved in the head of a big old grey rat, probably several months ago judging by the look of it.

The entire back wall of the room had been peppered with rusting four inch nails. Beneath each nail was a grey greasy stain tinged with red.

There was an old sofa in the middle of the room and a chest of drawers like the ones his grandma used to have with three big heavy wooden, brass handled drawers that came out easily but required advanced wrestling skills to push back in again.

There was no TV set or radio. Nothing worth stealing then. That didn't matter to Billy. He was here for the cash.

A large portion of the carpet was missing in one corner of the room. That had probably been where all the rubbish was stacked, Billy reasoned. The carpet would have been scraped off the floor and dumped or burned.

The floorboards were wide and seemed to be well nailed down. Billy had assumed that one of them at least would be loose to facilitate easy access to the stash. He pushed back the sofa. It made his hands feel greasy.

He started to peel back the carpet, rolling it up as he went. Success depended on him being able to put everything back as it was so that no-one even suspected that he'd been there.

Having moved everything out of the way he surveyed the floorboards looking for gaps or distortions. He soon found what he was looking for.

Just beneath where the sofa had been was an area where the joint between the boards was a little wider than the rest and on closer inspection there were fine cut lines across the planks. There was no doubt that this was some kind of trapdoor. He tried to work his fingers into the gap between the boards but it was too narrow. He went back into the kitchen and returned with a handful of cutlery to use as levers.

When he forced a knife into the gap and levered backwards, the board came up. He pushed his fingers under the board and lifted out the entire two feet square trapdoor. He put his head through the hole to look around but it was pitch black.

He cursed himself for being unprepared and went to the chest of drawers, pulling out each one in search of a lighter, or anything that would do the same job. He rummaged around in the middle drawer and found a very small torch. It lit up when he pushed the switch but the light was a pallid yellow colour. The batteries were almost done but it might hold out for five minutes or so.

He knelt on the floor and shone the torch into the hole. The ground was further down than he'd expected, possibly two and a half feet below the boards. It smelled earthy and damp as he leaned further in and shone the light around. There was nothing directly below the hole but as he cast the torchlight around under the house he caught sight of a small parcel wrapped inside a plastic carrier bag that had been thrown to the far end of the house. His heart leapt.

He pulled his head out of the hole in the hope that there might be another access point in the floor but was disappointed. He sighed deeply. He was going to have to go down there.

Billy wasn't a big man but he still found the hole a bit of a squeeze. He had to wriggle, snake like into the darkness and then lay on the damp earth fumbling in his pocket for the torch. Once orientated towards the parcel he set off at a bit of a crawl. The ground seemed to rise as he progressed and he soon found that he was reduced to inching himself along on his belly.

He was perhaps eight feet from the parcel when the torch began to fade. He banged it hard against the palm of his hand and it got momentarily brighter before dimming again. He carried on, now barely able to see but knowing that he didn't have far to go.

After a further thirty seconds of effort he finally got there. He reached out and grabbed the bag. The contents felt like blocks of paper. Leo had been telling the truth. As he started to work his way backwards the torch went out plunging him into darkness. He banged the torch on the ground twice but it didn't recover.

He felt the parcel suddenly torn from his grip.

'Fuck! Fuck! What the hell?' He gasped into the blackness, panic rising in his chest.

He tried to turn over but there wasn't room. Behind him something moved. He fought to turn himself around to face the way he'd come but it took monumental effort. He couldn't seem to catch his breath.

'It's just rats.' He tried to convince himself, his chest heaving. 'Just rats.'

He banged the torch again and the light flickered on, a feeble lack lustre beam that alighted on an old brown shoe. He brushed it aside and tried to move around further. His hands scraped at the dirt in an effort to pull him forward and he uncovered more clothing, and then bones.

Lots of bones.

Rat bones, dog bones, cat, chicken and unmistakeably human bones. He flew into a complete panic. Screaming loudly and fighting for breath he dragged himself onward toward the trapdoor. Each time he inched forward, slamming his hands to the ground, the torch light dimmed.

He was so close now, almost there. Just ten seconds of effort.

The torch went out.

Billy was spurred on by fear. Adrenalin tore through him as the ground lowered away and he found himself almost able to crawl. He was laughing with relief as he looked up toward the trapdoor.

His breath froze as he stared upward.

There were eyes. Hundreds of glassy, white eyes.

***

As Leo McDonald sat in his old armchair watching his favourite badly written soap opera his disjointed thoughts turned to Billy.

He's a good lad that Billy. Leo mused. Lola would like him. A bit skinny though, but then Lola always ate far too much.

*****

About the author.

John Vault is an Englishman abroad in New Zealand. He has produced several prize winning written works and fully intends to continue doing so. Writing for him has evolved from a means of escapism into something of an obsession. A subject that plays a major part in the content of many of his stories.

His writing style is unorthodox and rarely sticks firmly to the genre for which it is presented. The reader is often called upon to flip rapidly between gory horror and farcical comedy, enjoying a level of contrast that seeks to amplify the effect of both. His rampant use of expletives in character dialogue is also something of a trade mark and he makes no excuses for this other than blaming the characters themselves who are prone to adopting real lives for the short time that it takes to put their stories onto the page.

Outwardly he appears a normal man, having a wife, children and several household pets. Inwardly however he is a dark and cavernous soul who delights in gory horror and tales of insanity, fear and death. His stories are rarely formulaic and never truly just. Sometimes the hero and the villain are the same character. Sometimes the villains win and the heroes meet with ghastly deaths. This is the fun part, for what is the point of sowing the seeds of inner discord only to destroy them before they have the chance to truly blossom?

John welcomes any sincere comment on his work and is happy to talk to readers about any aspect of it. He can be reached via his publisher at:

Spinetinglers Publishing.
22 Vestry Road, Co. Down
BT23 6HJ UK
www.spinetinglerspublishing.com

Coming soon...

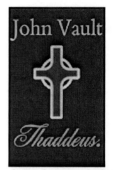

Thaddeus.

'Death is as popular now as it's always been...'

Hector Crane is a funeral director with no-one to bury. Business is at a standstill, he's on the verge of bankruptcy and his delinquent apprentices are stealing both from him and his dear departed clients.

Just when he thinks things can't get any worse he receives a letter from a man whom he thought long dead, who owns half of his business, and who will be knocking on his door very soon looking for answers.

Enter Thaddeus Moribund, who by Hector's reckoning should be at least ninety years old but appears half that, and who will overturn every aspect of Hector's life in a bid to pull the business through.

But there's immeasurably more to Thaddeus than this. His story unfolds in a series of revelations that span two millennia, beginning in biblical Jerusalem and ending in modern day England.

Thaddeus Moribund is on a mission of his own that has nothing to do with Hector Crane but which will nonetheless challenge Hector's patience, his strength, his concept of good and evil and finally his sanity as the connection between them is ultimately revealed.

'Am I right in thinking that... you actually intend to eat him?'

Thaddeus by John Vault.

ISBN: 978-1-906755-18-8

Uncle John's Bedtime Tales is also available for Kindle, Kobo, Nook and Sony Reader.

Produced in electronic format by HiRisc Publications and available from the following eBook online retailers:

www.smashwords.com
www.diesel-ebooks.com
www.kobobooks.com
www.amazon.com
www.amazon.co.uk
www.barnesandnoble.com

eISBN: 978-0-473-18131-4

CPSIA information can be obtained at www.ICGtesting.com
Printed in the USA
BVOW08s1336041013

332808BV00001B/27/P